MAGIC & MINT MARTINIS

EMILY MICHEL

Cover by Susan Renee from Jack'd Up Book Covers

For Breanna and Petra.
You reminded me just how much I love a spicy romcom.

AUTHOR'S NOTE

This book contains explicit language, explicit sexuality, alcohol use, mention of vomit, brief descriptions of past anti-fat bias, and current but brief struggles with internalized anti-fat bias.

The author welcomes feedback if you discover any further content that should be addressed in this note.

If you want to stay informed of the latest releases, get sneak peeks at works in progress, and get free short stories, please sign up for the Magical Musings Newsletter at:
www.EmilyMichelAuthor.com/newsletter.

Chapter 1
The Giggling Gaggle

If he had to listen to that Mariah Carey song one more time, Dash was going to lose his shit. Why had he agreed to work the bar tonight? Right, the regular bartender was on maternity leave. He swiped the rag across the bar near the giggling gaggle of bachelorettes who batted their eyelashes at him.

"Can I get you ladies anything?" he asked, knowing he would regret the answer.

The bride, wearing a plastic tiara with a short white veil hanging over her dark brown hair, slid up to the bar and tried to sit on a barstool. She missed and fell to the floor with a screech. He had to give the bridesmaids credit, they instantly turned their attention from him to their friend sprawled under his bar.

Despite their inebriated state and the bride's insistence on rising to her feet by herself, they managed to deposit her safely on the stool with only a minimum amount of squealing. Thank god. Between the high notes Ms. Carey hit and these beautiful, but too high-pitched, women, he was going to need a hearing check at the end of the night.

"Another round, bartender!" the bride shouted, slamming

her martini glass on the bar. The little candy cane went flying and landed in his hair.

With a sigh, he pulled it out and tossed it in the trash. Before he could say no, the sleigh bells over the entrance rang out merrily, and a woman pushed her way in. She was wrapped in a puffy down coat, a thick knit cap pulled low on her head, and a scarf wrapped around her throat. Fluffy snowflakes clung to her outerwear.

The bridesmaids were way too happy to greet this new customer for her to be a stranger. They bounced on their toes and the bride's smile widened, but tears appeared in the corners of her eyes.

"Lina! You made it!"

She tried to lunge at the newcomer, but the others propped her on the stool. The way-too-bundled-up Lina started unraveling her winter garb. First the scarf, bright red, wrapped at least three times around her neck, covering her nose.

Dash had seen plenty of beautiful women in this industry. They were a dime a dozen, including the nickel's worth currently in front of him. But Lina's rosy cheeks, pretty pink cupid's bow, and slightly pointy chin were perfectly balanced.

Next came the hat, a silly striped job that looked homemade with the largest green pom on top he'd ever had the honor of seeing, revealing a bunch of dark brown curls circling her head in a wreath, wild from the static.

The bachelorettes allowed the bride to leave her stool, and she immediately swept Lina into her sloppy hug, before plopping a tiara reading "Maid of Honor" on her head.

"Of course I made it, despite the airline's best efforts to delay me." Lina patted the other woman's back gently. "It's not every day your sister gets married."

He saw the resemblance, though the bride was taller with straight hair. And her lips weren't quite the same perfect pink.

But the biggest difference were the eyes. While the bride had perfectly respectable, even lustrous, warm brown eyes, Lina's were hazel, all greenish brown.

She shrugged off her puffy coat, revealing a body full of luscious curves begging to be explored. Shoving her hat, scarf, and gloves into the sleeve, she hung it on the hook at the end of the bar.

"So, what did I miss?" Lina took the stool next to her sister.

The bride returned to the bar, reminded in her drunken state of her mission to become even more so.

"We were about to order another round," she said.

Dash arched a brow. "And I was about to say no. You've had plenty."

"But my sister just showed up, she had the worst trip, and I haven't seen her in over a year. Please?" She pouted and batted her lashes.

He glanced at the new arrival.

"We're all catching a rideshare, so one more isn't going to hurt," Lina said.

"Fine, but only one more." Dash winked at Lina as the bridal party erupted into applause.

She blinked in surprise, but he turned away before she could say anything. Why on Earth had he done that? He didn't wink at the ladies. He didn't initiate the flirting. Ever. Never had to. But a single look at this woman, and he was hornier than a reindeer in rut.

He got busy making the drinks, six this round. Chocolate liqueur, creme de menthe, some cream, shaken over ice and garnished with a little, bitty candy cane.

Dash slid the last drink in front of Lina, who seemed a million miles away staring at her sister, but not really seeing her.

"Candy cane for your thoughts," he said.

She gave her head a little shake, sending all those curls into a frenzy. They looked as soft and silky as a snowshoe hare in the summer, and he wanted to run his hands through them. What was wrong with him today?

Lina considered the glass in front of her with those perfect lips pursed and her smooth forehead wrinkled. She was cute when she was confused.

"What the fuck is this?"

"It's what your friends are drinking. Top shelf chocolate-mint martini."

She groaned but snatched it off the bar. Taking a deep sniff, the confusion changed into curiosity, and her brows rose.

"Doesn't smell half bad. Well, beggars can't be choosers." She swallowed it in a few gulps, humming appreciatively as she returned the glass to the bar. "Thanks, I needed that."

"Want another?" He smiled, trying to keep it friendly and not more…sensual.

"As long as I'm not paying, why the hell not?"

"Coming right up, Ms. Scrooge."

He turned his back on her protests that she wasn't a Scrooge. Dash found himself whistling as he shook another cocktail. He stopped as he realized what it was he whistled. The damn "All I Want for Christmas" song again. Son of a bitch.

He delivered the drink with a friendly smile. "Then what are you?"

"Tired. It took me over thirty-six hours to get here from Europe."

Dash winced, but the other bartender dropped a bucket of ice before he could reengage in conversation. Great, just great.

"Excuse me," he said.

By the time he helped clean the mess, the delightful Ms. Lina had joined the festive bride and bridesmaids on the dance floor, shaking their booties to a jazzy song about Santa Claus.

He couldn't tear away his gaze. Her delight was captivating.

It wasn't long before they all came back to the bar, but Lina ordered water for the gaggle.

"You're no fun," her sister pouted, and the rest of the bridesmaids muttered their agreement.

"If memory serves, there's a dress fitting in the morning. You don't want to be nursing a hangover in a brightly lit dress shop, do you?" she said, the good mother hen. "Drink your water. You'll thank me tomorrow."

The sister planted a kiss on Lina's cheek, leaving behind a streak of coral lipstick. "I'll thank you now. You're always looking out for me. I love you!"

Lina rolled her eyes, but her smile was genuine. "I love you, too."

The ladies drank their water and returned to the dance floor, but Lina stayed behind, nursing her water.

Dash slid her another martini. "On the house."

She looked at it skeptically. "What are you putting in these? Sweet drinks aren't usually my jam, but this goes down smooth."

He gave her his best panty-dropping smile, widening it when her cheeks flushed. It had earned him plenty of dates and invited more than his fair share of women to his bed.

"Trade secret, I'm afraid. Don't worry, I'll cut you off if you get too tipsy."

"Oh, that's not why."

Before he could gather more information, a blond bridesmaid approached.

"Why do you get one?" She pouted and pulled on Lina's arm.

"Because I got here late and had to spend way too long hurtling through the atmosphere in a metal tube." Lina rose from the barstool, finished her drink in a long gulp, and allowed the bridesmaid to lead her to the dance floor.

After a couple of songs, she extricated herself from the crowd and returned to the bar, her hair even curlier with sweat, her cheeks even more flushed. What he wouldn't give to be the man making her flushed and sweaty. He readied another drink and met her as soon as she eased onto the barstool.

"Are you just hanging out waiting for me?" Lina sipped her drink and studied him.

Once again, he blessed her with his megawatt smile. Her pupils dilated and she licked her lips. Holy holly. He shifted closer to the bar so she wouldn't notice the boner her little gesture gave him.

"The boss and I have an arrangement. I'm allowed to keep the pretty women company."

She propped her elbow on the bar and rested her chin on her fist. Her gaze was slightly out of focus. That would be her last martini.

"Nice boss."

"Yeah, he's okay." Dash dragged the bar rag over the hard surface.

The crowd thinned, and he was about thirty minutes from ringing the last call bell. But he was loath to do anything to make this delectable creature leave before absolutely necessary.

"You remind me of someone." Lina blinked at him slowly, her long lashes fanning out.

He doubted she wore much makeup, and her lashes were not fake. It was truly an overabundance of lashes, ones he would like to examine in more detail as she slept beside him.

Dash pulled himself away from these thoughts. Ridiculous. He was being ridiculous tonight. He wasn't averse to settling down, but he enjoyed his single life. Maybe it was the change in schedule. Maybe it was her way of paying attention without sizing him up for a tux and an altar. Or was it—no, it couldn't be that.

He leaned in close enough to notice the tiny flecks of gold nestled in her irises like lights on a Christmas tree. "Who do I remind you of?"

Underneath the mint from the drink was a scent bringing to mind cinnamon and cayenne, her scent. It was all he could do to keep from inhaling deeply, *sniffing* her. That didn't fly in the modern world.

"Not sure, but it's almost as if I should know you." Lina finished her drink, maintaining eye contact. "Did we meet in elementary school or at summer camp?"

"I must have one of those faces." He did get that a lot, but he knew why. Before he had a chance to pull the conversation in a less dangerous direction, the gaggle swarmed her.

"C'mon, Lina," the sister said, slinging her arm around Lina's shoulder. "We're heading to the condo for popcorn and a movie marathon!"

The blond bridesmaid who dragged Lina to the dance floor earlier gestured for the tab and signed the bill.

"Thanks!" Dash glanced at the check.

Great tip, but written below her name was, "Call me anytime," with a phone number and an obscene number of hearts. She winked at him, then helped the bride into her coat. There were two or three with their phones out, trying to find rideshares while half drunk. Dash gently extricated one of the devices and helped. The women stumbled out the front door, and a little spark of chivalry made him slip his jacket on and follow them out into the softly falling snowflakes.

With six of them, they had called two cars, and Lina had taken charge, splitting them evenly. The first car took off, and she opened the front door to the second car.

"Goodnight, and happy holidays." A sad longing clawed at Dash's innards.

She looked at him, but her smile quickly faded, and she turned a pastel pea green. Before Dash could recoil, she puked all over his black boots. She wiped her mouth on the back of her glove.

"That's why I don't drink sweet drinks," she muttered.

"Jesus, lady—" the driver began.

"Oh, she's fine," her sister piped up from the back seat. "One and done, right, Lina?"

"Yeah." She turned those Christmas-tree irises to Dash. "I'm so, so sorry."

He waved it away. "It's not the first time somebody's puked on my boots. I'll keep it in mind if I ever serve you a drink again."

With a wan smile, she shut the door and the rideshare took her away. He wouldn't bump into her again, and unlike every other bar bunny who flirted with him, unlike all his one-night stands, it affected him deeply. More like the endings of his, what one—no, two long-term relationships. For a woman he'd spent all of twenty minutes with total.

Dash went around to the alley, asked the kitchen for some water, and did his best washing the vomit off his boots while trying to figure out why.

"Some night, boss," the cook said as he made his way through the kitchen.

"Yeah, but what are you gonna do? Keep the pretty ladies away?"

A bunch of protests followed him and he pushed through the kitchen door to the bar. The other bartender shook his head.

"You're too nice, Dash. If I was the boss, I woulda cut them off earlier."

"What can I say, I'm a softy." He rang the last call bell. "Pay up, Massholes!"

The regulars all grumbled, but tabs were paid, coats were donned, and in a few minutes, the bar was empty except for staff.

"Hey, boss," the other bartender said, "I've got finals on Monday and need to study. Can I take off now?"

"Fine, fine. Go. And good luck."

He really was turning into a softy. Was it only being nice to pay his people what they were worth and give them a break when all they were trying to do was better themselves? No. It was good business in the long run. He had half the turnover rate as most other bars and clubs in the city, and he promoted from within his growing business. You might start as a twenty-year-old server at The Old Bell, but you could finish as an executive vice president at Nichols Entertainment before your thirty-fifth birthday. It had happened to at least four people in the past fifteen years, and he was just getting started.

Soon enough the bar was clean, the floors were mopped, and the prep done for tomorrow. Dash locked the door behind the last of the staff and turned off all the lights. Time to head home.

He pulled an odd silver skeleton key from his pocket. It sat cold in his palm, surrounded by a blue light. The bit, the part that unlocked the door, was in the shape of a snowflake. Dash returned to the door and a keyhole appeared, also glowing blue. The key fit perfectly, and the door frame blazed, casting the kitchen in an eerie shimmer. He twisted the key and the door disappeared. Tucking the key back into his pocket, he walked through the portal. As soon as he stepped through, the door in the bar would return to normal, as if the magic had never happened.

CHAPTER 2
A VERY PARTICULAR MEMORY

Lina had set the most annoying alarm she could on her phone, the old dog barking one. It still took a while for it to penetrate her killer hangover-jet lag combo. Why, oh why, had she consumed four—four!—chocolate-mint martinis? She knew better.

The door to her room slammed open.

"Good morning, sleepy head! As you so kindly pointed out, we have a dress fitting."

Sometimes she hated Cassie's unending optimism and ability to shake off almost any insult to her system. Hangovers, jet lag, head colds. Lina had two out of the three at the moment, and the last thing she wanted to do was try on a bridesmaid dress. But she had returned from her assignment to partake in all the festivities, both holiday and wedding, so she would go. But damned if she would enjoy it.

How was she even conscious after the last forty-eight hours? No, more. She'd woken at the butt crack of dawn three days ago to drive to Athens, only to discover her flight was delayed. She made it to London, where they flat-out canceled the leg to Boston. After two or three uncomfortable hours dozing as she waited for the next flight, she was too wired to sleep on the plane across the Atlantic. By the time she arrived at the bar last night, she was half-dead from exhaustion.

Oh, the bar. And the flirty bartender. As consciousness wormed its ugly way through her, a very particular memory surfaced.

"Hey, Cass, did I actually puke on the hot bartender?" *Oh, please say no. Please.*

Her sister giggled. "Just his boots. Glorious. Always can count on you to end the night with a bang, Lina."

She groaned and dragged the blankets back over her head. The man had been exactly her type with wavy auburn hair, a close-clipped beard, twinkling blue eyes, and cute little dimples when he smiled. Not too tall, not too short, muscular without looking as if he lived at the gym. And he seemed into her. Lina had considered returning once or twice during her visit the next three weeks, try to lure him into her bed. Any bed, really. Then she'd lost the martinis.

Cassie pulled the covers off her.

"Ugh, can't you let me die from embarrassment?" Lina threw her arm over her eyes.

"No way, Alice would make a horrible maid of honor. Come on. You're gonna love the dress I picked out for you."

Her mouth tasted like a cheap packet of mint cocoa powder had crawled in and died. Lina staggered to the bathroom down the hall and turned on the shower while brushing her teeth. The mere idea of anything other than coffee had her stomach protesting.

A few minutes later, clean and shiny and dressed in comfortable clothes—she owned nothing else—Lina sat at the kitchen counter, cupping her coffee in her hands.

Wesley, her sister's fiancé, pulled some toast from the toaster and placed it in front of her.

Lina pushed it away. "Thanks, Wes, but no thanks. No repeats on the show from last night."

"Trust me, Lina, Cassidy's friends are much easier to take with food in your belly." He flashed her his perfect smile, and his brown eyes lit up.

Wesley was tall, with short blond hair and chiseled cheekbones sharp enough to cut glass. Smooth shaven, he painted the perfect picture of a corporate lawyer. He rarely dressed in anything more casual than a button-down shirt and slacks.

Lina nibbled on the toast, and her stomach settled a bit.

"Good girl," he said.

She stuck out her tongue.

"Gross." He laughed and poured himself another cup of coffee.

"I didn't get a chance to say it last night but thank you for letting me crash here. It can't be easy having an interloper as the wedding approaches." She bit into the toast again, feeling much better.

"You're not an interloper, Lina, you're family. You'll always be welcome in our home."

He was handsome and rich *and* kind. Her sister had won the lottery.

"Still, thanks. With Mom and Dad in Arizona, and Granny…"

Lina choked up. She couldn't help it, even over a year later. Wesley patted her shoulder.

"Hey, family, right? And who wouldn't offer a place to stay for the do-gooder daughter of the Schultz family?"

"What am I, chopped liver?" Cassie walked in looking as put-together as always, wearing a pale blue wool sweater over a pinstriped Oxford shirt and gray slacks that hugged her hips like a second skin.

Lina wished she could find clothes to fit her that well. Her sister had inherited their father's long, lean frame, while Lina was the spitting image of their mother, average height and above average curves. Way above average. Fat, some would call her. In this late capitalist hellscape, most would mean it in a negative way.

But Lina had embraced her body for what it was long ago. It helped her family was body positive. No one ever warned her a moment on the lips was a lifetime on the hips. Both her parents taught her to make healthy choices in her food and to exercise. And her current job made both things all the more important, though it was hard some days to access fresh fruits and veggies.

The only thing she despaired of was finding off-the-rack clothes that made her feel as pretty as she was. She had no time to sew for herself, and since Granny had lost her eyesight years ago, there was no one else to sew for her. Relegated to the sometimes awful world of plus-size clothing, she did the best she could. She usually chose comfort over fashion anyway, but it would be nice to have more options.

Wesley poured Cassie a mug of coffee and passed it to her with a kiss more appropriate for the bedroom than the kitchen.

"Get a room," Lina said with a smirk.

Cassie let go with a giggle. "I'm sure if the hot bartender had kissed you like that last night, you wouldn't complain."

"No, but he might. I can't show my face there again."

Which was too bad. She could have used a fling. Work had kept her too busy to make it into the city much, and she needed a distraction with all the wedding and holiday preparations. And since flings were about all she could manage with her job taking her all around the world, she'd been looking forward to finding one. The bartender last night had been a prime candidate, until…

"Aren't you two going to be late?" Wesley looked at his smart watch.

"They can't start without the bride," Cassie said airily.

"Cass, they have a bunch of other brides to worry about. No need to muck up their day because we're hungover." Lina shoved the rest of her toast in her mouth and washed it down with the dregs in her cup.

With the ibuprofen kicking in, she was excited about today's fitting. Cassie had excellent taste, and Wesley's parents had insisted on an upscale bridal shop known for custom work. She sent her measurements months ago, and today was the final fitting, the tweaks to make sure it fit her just right.

"I was kidding." Cassie grabbed her bag and coat and headed for the door.

Lina snagged her coat from where she'd left it hanging over a chair last night. She pulled her scarf and gloves from the sleeve, but where was her hat? The hat Granny had knitted for her in high school? Oh no.

"What is it, Lina?" Wesley asked. "You look pale as a ghost."

"I lost my hat." Lina held back the tears.

"You can borrow my extra."

Cassie shook her head vigorously at him, making a slashing motion across her throat.

"What? It's a hat."

Cassie put her arms around Lina and glared at her fiancé in the most adorable way. "It's not just a hat, doofus. Granny made it for her in high school. Every Schultz has a ridiculous hat made by her."

Wesley joined in on the group hug and whispered in Lina's ear. "Sorry. Can I help you find it?"

"No." Hopelessness and embarrassment washed through her. "It's either in the rideshare or…"

"Oh no," Cassie said.

"Yep, might have to see a man about a hat and apologize for

puking on him. Again."

Time for a walk of shame. But first, dresses.

Chapter 3
No Fucking Tiaras

"Get up, Dash. You're late, and Dad's going to shit candy canes."

Dash groaned in pain. "Fuck off, Joy. It's too early for this."

"It's after noon, and you were supposed to be at the board meeting fifteen minutes ago."

His sister's blond curls and perky fucking nose came into focus. Dash tried to close his eyes again, but she grabbed his leg and pulled. It was either stand or collapse in a heap on the floor, and he couldn't let his little sister embarrass him.

Dash rose and stretched as if that was his plan all along.

"For chrissakes, put on some pants!" Joy stomped to the chair in the corner, grabbed the pair of pants draped across it, and threw them at his head.

Dash caught them but just stood there in his boxer briefs. Wasn't his fault his sister refused to respect his privacy.

"And take a shower. You smell like somebody puked an entire bottle of peppermint schnapps on you."

She wasn't far off.

"I'll have you know, they were top shelf chocolate-mint martinis." He dropped the pants on his bed. "And the ladies at the bar couldn't drink enough of them."

"Ugh, even worse. I covered for you, asshole. I told them you were out Christmas shopping and the lines were impossibly long. You owe me big time."

Dash hated owing his sister anything. The little twerp usually held it over his head for years, even after he paid up. He stumbled toward the bathroom. A shower sounded good, but he leaned against the doorframe to negotiate.

"So what do you want Santa to drop in your stocking this year?"

She tapped a finger to her lips, her blue eyes sparkling with mischievous mirth. "A tiara would be nice. Big and sparkly."

"No. No fucking tiaras." The shiny plastic accessories danced through his memory, especially the one marked "Maid of Honor" perched on a cloud of silky brown curls.

"Fine," she huffed. "A new car. Bright red, with the premium sound system."

He flipped her off as he closed the door to the bathroom. Maybe he should have caved on the tiara. How was he going to go car shopping over the next—was it only two weeks until Christmas? He had a restaurant empire to run, bar shifts to cover, and a beautiful woman to track down.

No, that was creepy. If the fates intended, he would find her again.

Dash wished he could stay a bit longer in the shower. If he had his druthers, it would be long enough to imagine what pretty Lina looked like under the fuzzy sweater and leggings she wore last night. How her breasts might feel in his hands. How she might taste, at least when not drinking those martinis he made last night. Mint had a tendency to overpower everything else.

He flipped the shower to cold and rinsed off. Explaining to the board why he showed up with a hard-on would be bad enough, but his dad was scheduled to make an appearance today. Despite turning forty this coming spring, he was not having an awkward conversation with his dad, not today.

Perhaps it was for the best Lina left without giving him her number. Humans often reacted clumsily at best, downright hostilely at worst, to the magical world. This way, he could have his fantasies at least.

He dressed in his usual black slacks and chose a blue sweater. The family business was a casual affair, except for one night each year. Dash hurried through the passageways of the complex until he arrived at the boardroom, smack dab in the center.

He walked in, apology on his lips. "Sorry I'm late. Traffic was bad."

Ah hell, it was supposed to be long lines.

Joy sat at the far end of the room, smirking as she shook her head. Next to her sat their mother, her silver-threaded auburn waves gathered loosely into a braided crown on her head. And next to Katja Nichols was the big guy himself.

His blond hair had turned white before Dash's twentieth birthday, but his dark blue eyes twinkled like stars in the midnight sky. His cheeks were round and rosy, and when he smiled, his dimples called everybody to join in his mirth.

But Ivan Nichols was not smiling. In fact, if it weren't for the ermine bedecked red velvet coat hung on his chair, no one would guess they were in the presence of Santa Claus himself.

The rest of the board waited on the edge of their seats for Ivan's response. Every last elf would react the way his father did. The pointy eared bastards were loyal, some to a fault.

He couldn't blame them. His father was good at what he did. Delivering presents to millions of children in less than twenty-four hours was a feat, even with elven magic. Ivan Nichols treated all elves with respect, from the newest arrivals to the retirees who still volunteered to take a load on the big night. He had modernized in ways Dash's grandfather never considered.

Dash had learned everything he knew about running a successful business from Santa himself. His father was a good teacher and an excellent boss. Dash waited for the boot to drop.

Surprisingly, his father said nothing, merely gestured to the empty chair on his left. Dash sat on the uncomfortable wooden chair that was older than dirt by a few millennia.

"Now we're all here, let's begin," Ivan announced in his rich baritone. "Stable?"

"Donner has an abscess on her left rear hoof. She's out for Christmas Eve, but I think Stanley is ready for his first flight," said the head groom, a woman who had an expert touch with the reindeer.

Joy held her chin high, a satisfied grin on her face. She'd handpicked Stanley last year to train. His sister had a knack for picking out promising members of the team, much like their grandfather.

"Excellent. Can't wait to work with our newest addition. Toys?"

A young elf, who seemed barely old enough to have graduated from college last spring, piped up. "We're good to go. No surprise last-minute must-haves this year, sir."

"Where's Cricket?" Ivan asked kindly.

The young elf gulped. "She's a bit indisposed, sir. She ate some store-bought cookies."

A gasp circled the table. Everybody knew of Cricket's food sensitivities. Most store-bought cookies were loaded with preservatives, which had a tendency to send her praying to the porcelain god. But at some point each Christmas season, she had to test the waters.

Dash made a mental note to visit her a bit later, take her some sparkling cider. That usually set her back to rights.

The reports kept coming, a half dozen in all. Except for the usual minor snafus, everything was in order. There should be no difficulty in putting a present under the tree for each child this year. The same as last year. The same as the year before. And the year before that…ad infinitum for the past several centuries.

Everybody had everything covered, so Dash checked out. He nodded when everybody else nodded. Sighed when his father did, and occasionally drummed his fingers on the table. But no matter how much he pretended to follow along, his mind kept drifting to his encounter with the fascinating and beautiful woman from last night. The way she smiled, the wild abandon she had on the dance floor, and how she brought a breath of fresh, snow-crisp air into his life for a shining moment.

Before long, the other elves were leaving. The only thing saying they weren't human were the ears. Same variation in height, weight, skin tones, hair color, eye color, but those pointy ears gave away the game. He hid his own pointed ears with a glamour he refreshed once a week whenever he needed to venture out into the human world.

"Dash, Earth to Dash." His father's voice called him back from his wandering thoughts.

"Yeah, Dad?"

"Why were you actually late?"

Of course, the man in charge of the naughty and nice list would realize he was lying.

Dash yawned. "Had to close last night. My head bartender is out on maternity leave."

"That is very kind of you," his mother said. "But you pay your staff well enough for one of them to cover, right?"

"I do, but I need to put in an appearance from time to time, not just to sign paperwork, but to really work. Show them I know what it's like."

Though his mom nodded earnestly, Joy rolled her eyes. She would be happy to never leave the North Pole if she could help it. Too bad their dad insisted on Dash taking the reins when he finally retired. Neither Dash nor Joy let it affect their relationship most of the time, but every once in a while, she tried to call her dad on this bullshit.

It hadn't worked yet.

"But you don't," his dad said. "They rely on you for their livelihood, but you wouldn't suffer at all if you never worked another day in your life. You'd always have a roof over your head here, plenty of food, and work to keep you busy."

Dash stood and paced to his favorite spot in the boardroom—a window seat his grandmother had insisted on installing for her grandchildren. He flopped down and huffed dramatically.

"I want something else, at least for now. I'll step in when it's time, and I swear I'm paying attention." Well, mostly. "And running my business will more than prepare me to run Christmas Eve when my turn rolls around, but I hope you live a good long life, and I won't have to do it for at least a century yet."

His dad was still a spry 102, so Dash had to find an activity to keep him busy. Thus, his string of clubs and bars. His favorite was The Old Bell from last night. Tucked away in an old Boston neighborhood, some of the most interesting people randomly appeared. Like lovely Lina.

His mom sat next to him and patted his shoulder. "He only hopes you follow in his footsteps."

"I know. And I will. Or Joy will. Either way, kids will still get gifts on Christmas, and the Santa Claus legacy will live on. I promise."

"You're right," his dad said, "there's plenty of time, and your business experience will only help when you take over. We just miss you."

Dash made it a point to attend family dinner at least once a week, and he was there for all the major holidays. He did his part and did it well, but there wasn't a lot to do. He was a man who needed his own purpose in his life, separate from his family.

"I'm here. I don't know what else I can do," he said.

His dad gripped his shoulder. "You'll figure it out. Will you be at dinner tonight?"

"Afraid not. Got another shift to cover."

"Tomorrow?"

"Definitely tomorrow." Dash assured his dad and was blessed with those merry dimples, the same ones he had.

His dad grabbed his coat and left, Joy trailing behind him. Since her lie hadn't worked, did he still owe her a car? He could buy her a toy car, make it into a premium speaker for her phone. That would cover the bases, wouldn't it?

"What's her name?"

He jumped. "Oh for…Mom, don't sneak up on a guy."

"You didn't answer my question."

"What makes you think there's a woman?"

"I haven't seen you this dreamy since what's-her-name in college. Veronica? No, Valerie."

"Victoria. Her name was Victoria."

His relationship with Victoria had caused a whole host of issues, each falling like a domino until the only solution was a desperate one. Since then, he'd dated much more casually, waiting. For what, he wasn't sure, but he would know when he found it.

"Well, what's her name?"

"There isn't a woman this time."

He would not tell his mother about the lascivious fantasies featuring Lina. He'd only met her yesterday and spent less than thirty minutes in her presence. It was just a little infatuation. With somebody he would never meet again, more's the pity.

"Uh-huh." His mother stood on tiptoes and kissed his cheek. "Have fun tonight."

She danced out of the room. Somehow, his mother always seemed to dance.

Dash pulled out the key and opened the portal to the office in the bar. What holiday surprises might be in store tonight? As long as it didn't end with vomit again, it would be a good night.

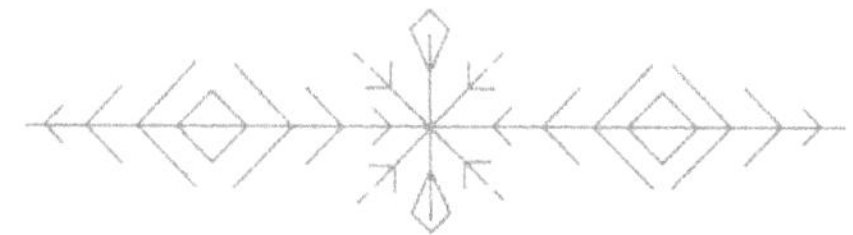

Chapter 4
Some Sort of Christmas Miracle

Sleigh bells sang out as Lina opened the door. A couple of heads turned her way, but at four in the afternoon, it seemed the bar was filled with regulars who had learned to ignore the sound of the bells. Lina wasn't sure she would ever be able to ignore them. The perfectly tuned jingle sent the good kind of shivers down her spine. The kind that tempted her to sing along, and dance, and laugh.

If Christmas could be distilled to a single sound, it would be those bells.

The bartender from last night wasn't there. Relief flooded her system. It was bad enough to have to come back and look for her hat. She would probably expire from embarrassment if she ever had to face him again. There was a moment last night, before the unfortunate incident, where she had a shot. But there was no way now. What man in his right mind asked out someone who puked on him? A shame—he ticked all her boxes for a home-for-the-holidays hookup.

An older woman greeted her as Lina unwound her scarf and brushed snowflakes from her hair.

"What can I get you?"

"I was here last night, and I think I left my hat behind."

"Oh, sure. Let me grab the lost and found from the office."

Lina plonked her ample ass on a barstool and fiddled with a cocktail napkin. She froze when a rich, deep voice seeped from behind the kitchen door. Before her brain's signal to run made it through her fear response, *he* walked through, carrying a cardboard banker's box.

Mr. Bartender himself, with his sweet dimples and effervescent baby blues, set the box down and looked at her. His eyes widened, and a slow smile crept across his mouth, which sent an entirely different kind of shiver along her spine. The kind that tempted her to rip off her clothes and dance naked in the moonlight. She'd felt this odd sensation once or twice in her life, yet despite the rush of hormones and her thundering heart, there was something perfectly right about it, about him.

"Well hello, Lina. I didn't expect to see you again so soon."

All the blood rushed up her neck to settle in her cheeks. She must have resembled Rudolph's nose, all shiny and bright red. Lina limply waggled her fingers at him.

"Um, hi…you know, I never caught your name last night."

He stuck his hand out, the grin never leaving his lips. "Dash Nichols."

She took it. "Lina Schultz. And I want to apologize again, for, well…"

Dash squeezed her hand gently, wonder flashing across his face so fast she almost missed it as he let go.

"Hey, don't mention it. Please."

She bit her lip, and his gaze focused on the small movement, like a kid staring at the biggest marshmallow in a cup of cocoa.

"Thanks," she murmured.

He cleared his throat and pulled the lid off the banker's box. "So, Julia said you're looking for your hat. It had a big green pom, right?"

His Spanish accent on Julia's name was perfect, pronouncing the J as an H. And he remembered the color of the pom on her hat.

"Yes. It's just a hat, but my granny made it for me in high school. Sentimental value."

"It's not in here. I'm sorry."

Lina sniffed and dug her fingernails into her palms. She was not going to cry over a hat. She wasn't. She had all sorts of things Granny had made for her and more than enough memories to last a lifetime. It was just a hat.

"Oh no, don't cry."

He encased her hands in his before she could move, and peace fell over her. She still grieved eighteen months later, and losing the hat brought it all back. But her anguish over losing the woman who had always been in her corner, no matter what, who always had something warm to wrap her in, be it a hug or a hat, who had loved her fiercely and told her every goddamned day, was soothed away in his gentle touch.

Lina looked deep into his eyes, blue as the winter sky on a cold, clear day, and a different emotion sparked. She would give anything to stare into those eyes for a bit longer, like a night, or eternity. Yeah, eternity might do.

She blinked. Eternity? She wasn't an eternity kind of gal. Her job kept her far from home and made it difficult to settle down, let alone have a long-term relationship. The strange feeling vanished, but the peace remained. She no longer had to fight her tears anymore; she no longer needed to cry.

"Thank you," she whispered.

Dash had a thousand-yard stare, but her words drew him back to the here and now.

"I didn't do anything. Couldn't even find your hat." He kept hold of her hands.

"Yeah, but..." Lina didn't know how to finish the sentence.

Thanks for holding my hands? Thanks for the moment of peace? Thanks for not making me feel like a twit? "Thanks for looking."

"Anytime. Did you check with the rideshare yet?" He finally, reluctantly, let go of her and recovered the box.

"Yes. No joy."

Lina rose from the barstool. The hat wasn't here, nor was it with the rideshare. She wasn't getting her hat back.

"If you want..." He cleared his throat and his cheeks pinkened, the barest touch of red. "You could leave your number, and if it turns up, I can call you."

Teenage Lina would be skeptical—no way a guy this hot could possibly be asking her out. Twenty-something Lina would have taken him precisely at his word. But thirty-two-year-old Lina had lived, laughed, and loved, and this guy was attracted to her. She would bet everything in her savings account, all $1,367, on it.

She pushed away the urge to smile. Maybe this holiday trip home would have some extra special benefits. "Sure. Thanks."

He passed her a scrap of paper and a pen, and she scribbled down her number.

"No problem." He took the paper and tucked it into his pocket.

She walked to the door and turned. "And, you know, you could call anyway."

Before he could respond, she opened the door and walked away.

Holy crap, she had given her number to the hottest man she'd ever had the chance to be in the same room with, told him to call her, and had every expectation he would. What the hell was happening to her this year? Some sort of Christmas miracle?

Lina didn't dare think too hard on it. She hurried to the subway—nope, she was home—the T and headed to her sister's condo.

CHAPTER 5
VISIONS OF LINA

The phone number burned a hole in Dash's pocket. He kept slipping his hand in to touch it, reassure himself it was real. How long was too long to wait to call her? How soon was too soon? Was now good?

What was going on? He was never this nervous around women, but Lina did things to him. Made him feel sixteen all over again. Made him yearn to stick around and just take her in. Listen to her voice. Stare into her eyes. Take her home and introduce her to his parents.

He had introduced one woman to his parents in his life. To say it was a disaster would be an understatement of monumental proportions. Victoria had freaked once she realized he wasn't as human as she naturally assumed. Thank god for elvish magic. A little spell on some mulled wine, and she forgot he was the son of Santa. And a few days later, he broke up with her. It had almost broken his heart. Almost.

When he shook Lina's hand, a zing of energy had traveled from her to him and straight into his brain. Brains, actually, the big one and the little one. And when he held her hands, he could nearly read her thoughts. She had been so sad, and all he wanted was to give her a moment of peace. Somehow he had.

"You should call her," Julia said. "It's obvious you're into each other."

"Really? How obvious?"

She snorted. "Like I was about ready to suggest you take her to the office for a little quiet…um, let's call it conversation."

If she had said anything of the sort, he would have done it. There was nothing he desired more than to spend some quality time with Lina Schultz. The rest of his life sounded good.

He needed to approach his mother. She could confirm what was going on, but it would have to wait. Julia was off the clock in another hour. Tomorrow, first thing.

After Julia left, his newest hire arrived. Though the new guy was grasping the tricks of the trade quickly, he was still learning. Dash ran between the bar, the kitchen, and his office more times than he could count, putting out figurative fires. And a literal one when the oil in a pan ignited. He had never moved so quickly in his life, but no harm done.

This was why he loved the restaurant business. Never a dull moment. With so many jobs to do—accounting, bartending, marketing, interior design, graphic design, cooking, he could go on—there was much to learn and new challenges cropped up all the time.

While satisfying in many ways, the Santa business was dull, at least to Dash. Modern technology had made everything and everybody at the North Pole super-efficient. There wasn't much for him to do besides make toys, except in the weeks leading to Christmas. Even then, his dad had implemented systems which kept all the cogs well-oiled. Joy thrived, but Dash preferred the chaos of the food service industry.

After helping the new guy close, Dash headed home and collapsed into bed a bit after midnight, with visions of Lina dancing through his head.

He woke without the help of his snotty little sister late the next morning. Dash padded to the kitchen to find coffee and something to eat. His mother puttered around, prepping dinner. Already, tantalizing smells wafted through the air. It made the muesli he was about to have for breakfast a poor substitute.

"Good morning, Mom." He kissed her cheek before pouring a steaming cup from the thermal carafe, which was always full and hot thanks to elven magic.

"Good morning, dear. Didn't hear you come in last night." She stirred a fragrant concoction on the stove.

"Headed straight to my room." He added a little sugar and rummaged in the pantry for the muesli.

"You're working too hard."

"The head bartender for The Old Bell is out on maternity leave."

"Oh, that's right. You mentioned it the other day. How is she doing?"

"Baby was born three days ago, and they're both doing great."

His mother went all misty-eyed and opened her mouth. He didn't need to be reminded about his duty to provide the next generation of Santas. He was still young by elf standards. Not even forty, when he could expect to live nearly another 150 years. But his mother loved kids, especially babies. She spent most of her time in the North Pole nursery looking after all the elflings too young for school. Nothing would make her happier than a grandchild or ten.

"Don't say it, Mom. It will happen or it won't, on its own schedule."

Honestly, he'd never considered having kids of his own. He wasn't opposed to them, but the idea hadn't crossed his mind. Now that Lina had entered the picture…the idea became more appealing.

"A mother can hope."

He poured milk over his cereal and sat at the small table in the corner of the kitchen. Most family meals happened here, but he and Joy were both grown, and they were less frequent. Dash both relished more freedom from his family and regretted not spending more time with them. He moved the cereal around with his spoon without eating a bite.

His mother put the lid on the pot, set the spoon to the side, and wandered over.

"What is it?" She slid onto a seat.

"What's what?"

"You're too quiet, and you haven't eaten yet. That's not like you."

He needed to talk to her but didn't want to get her hopes up. After all, he'd only spoken to Lina twice. It was more a gut instinct than anything at this point. But he had to know.

Between his father and his mother, he would much rather broach such a sensitive subject with his mom. Ivan Nichols was a bit old school—more likely to glower or yell—while his mom always had a hug and a smile for him.

"What's the helpmate bond like?"

His parents were one of the few mated couples he knew, and the only one he could easily talk to. The next best option was a distant cousin he'd never gotten along with.

His mother's eyes sparkled, but she wisely refrained from asking why. A wistful smile quirked up her lips.

"It's like coming home. Being around the person is calming, and you sense deep in your heart there is no one else for you."

That wasn't quite how it was. In fact, the calming part was all wrong. He felt anything but *calm*. What he desired to do was kiss her senseless, rip off her clothes, and bury himself deep inside her. Best keep those thoughts to himself, yet there was a deep-seated *belonging* when he was near her.

"But what about when you first meet them?"

She cleared her throat and covered his hands with her own.

"Sure you want me to tell you? It involves things most people don't want to know about their parents."

"Ew."

"There's a powerful physical attraction at first. Once you, um…"

"Mom!"

"Well, you're almost forty, and you haven't been celibate."

He dropped his forehead on the table and stared at his slippered feet. He might have to listen to his mother talk about this, but he wasn't going to look her in the eye while she explained.

"Once you've explored that aspect of the relationship…" Dash heard the barely contained laughter in his mother's voice. Glad this amused somebody. Why, oh why, had he asked? "…it settles into this sense of rightness. You're the best possible version of yourself when they're around. There's nothing you can't do, as long as this person loves you. And there's nothing you wouldn't do to protect them from anything and everything causing them harm or distress."

Oh, yeah, that's why he asked. Because two brief conversations, an hour tops, with Lina had upended his life. Now he had to convince her to feel the same and to believe in Santa Claus again, or risk losing this chance at abiding love.

"What…what happens if the helpmate doesn't return the feelings? Or decides not to pursue them for whatever reason?"

He looked up. Concern replaced his mother's wistful and impish expression.

"I don't know. In all of elvish history, I can't remember anyone ever rejecting their helpmate."

Dash couldn't bring himself to warn his mother he suspected his helpmate was human. That was another crappy gift he refused to open at the moment. Maybe this was only a strong infatuation. Maybe if he invited her on a date, he would learn she was all wrong for him. And maybe Rudolph's nose wouldn't glow this year.

"Thanks, Mom."

He tried to pull away, but she was having none of it.

"Dash, is there something you wish to tell me?"

"Not yet. I swear I will when there is anything to tell."

She let him go. "Okay. You know where to find me."

"One more thing—can you not tell Dad yet? Or Joy." Definitely not Joy. He couldn't stand the teasing.

"Of course. What's there to say, anyway?"

Katja Nichols returned to stirring whatever was in her pot, and Dash shuffled to his room with another cup of coffee.

He pulled out the phone number and dialed.

CHAPTER 6
HOTTIE MCBARTENDER

The phone vibrated its way across the kitchen island. Lina grabbed for it as it started to fall. It was lunch on a Sunday. She had already talked to her parents. And what area code was that? Canada?

She hesitated. Probably a scammer, but a niggling voice in the back of her mind told her she needed to take this call.

"Hello?"

"Lina?" Her sexy bartender's voice came through. Dash.

She couldn't believe it. In what world did the hot bartender call her? *This one, silly.* There was a connection between them, and she deserved to find out what it was, have a little fun while she was home. Experience had proven that was all she could expect, anyway.

Breathlessly, she said, "Yes."

"It's Dash. Listen, I still haven't found your hat but hoped you wouldn't mind if I called."

Lina bit her lip and squashed the urge to giggle like an airhead. "It's fine. I'm glad you did."

"Wonderful!"

His deep voice hit all the right places. Her blood thrummed

with possibility.

"Are you busy tomorrow night?" he continued.

With her job taking her to the far corners of the world, she was maid of honor in name only. The wedding planner hired by Wesley's wealthy parents was doing most of the work, and Cassie's best friend had arranged the bachelorette party and bridal shower, which Lina had missed two months ago. All Lina had to do was show up for these events and go to the dress fitting.

Though she'd taken almost all her vacation time to help with the final stages of a New Year's Eve wedding and spend time with her family for the holidays, her job was mostly done. She had a few Christmas presents to buy and wrap, and some minor wedding errands before the big day.

"No, I am not."

"Care to join me for dinner?"

"I would love to." She tried to keep her voice casual, but she was pretty sure she failed. She hadn't been this giddy about a date since her first one in college.

"Do you have any preferences? Or any dietary restrictions?"

"Dietary restrictions?" What was he asking?

"Yeah, like are you vegan? Any food allergies?"

"Oh, no. Nothing like that. I'll eat almost anything."

She cringed inwardly. A woman her size bragging about what she'll eat. No, she'd worked too hard to get to this place. And it was the truth. Her travels, her job, had broadened her palate. She had eaten and enjoyed things in the past few years that Lina from college didn't even know could be food.

"Is this your cell? I can make reservations and text you the details."

"Yes, sounds good. Just keep it within easy walking distance from a T station." Not a huge requirement. Boston had an extensive public transportation system.

"I can do that." His smile came through his voice, and

another lovely shiver of anticipation coursed through her. "I'll see you tomorrow."

"See you tomorrow."

In a trance-like state, she hung up and placed the phone on the counter. Of course, her sister chose then to sweep into the room.

"Who was that?" Cassie's voice was high and sickeningly sweet.

Lina remained silent, her brain still catching up to the fact the world's most gorgeous bartender had asked her out on a date.

"Lina?" Cassie shook her shoulder. "Carolina Schultz, what's wrong?"

"I have a date."

Her sister blinked at her. "A date? With who?"

"The guy whose boots I puked on."

"Hottie McBartender? Oh my god, Lina, that's fantastic!"

Cassie hugged her tight. Still, Lina didn't react.

"It *is* fantastic, right?" Cassie examined her from head to toe.

"Yeah, but what am I going to wear? All I have are leggings and sweaters! I don't even have a dress for the rehearsal dinner yet, and the bridesmaid's dress won't be ready for another week and a half."

"You have plenty of time to shop."

True. She still had Christmas presents to buy. She'd brought some souvenirs from her latest assignment, small things that were easy to fit into luggage. And there was a little room in her budget for a nice outfit or two. She could store them here with Cassie for her next trip home.

"You're right. I do. Do I have time for a haircut, too?"

There weren't many hair stylists in the rural areas she was often assigned, so she wore it short and got a trim whenever she made it home. Her last haircut had been before a series of in-country meetings in the big city this past summer. She was well overdue.

"Yes, I'll call the salon first thing tomorrow and make sure they squeeze you in. They're doing all the wedding day hair. Ooh, I'm so excited for you."

Lina rubbed her ears as her sister's voice hit a register only dogs could hear. "Yeah, I can tell."

They exploded into giggles. It had been so long since Lina had a proper date, at least two years. She always managed a hookup or two whenever she visited home, but her last actual date had been in Athens with a colleague before they received their final assignments. His had kept him in the city while she'd gone to the rural area where her expertise was more needed.

There weren't many men willing to try a long-distance relationship with an international aid worker who was gone for months at a time. Even fewer were patient enough to stick it out when her assignments took her far from the modern conveniences of Wi-Fi and regular mail service. So Lina had quit trying to find a long-term relationship, but at least this trip home she would have a shot at a hot-and-heavy liaison with Mr. McBartender.

"You can't tell Mom and Dad, Cassidy. You know how they get. It's just a date, and even if there's the kernel of a relationship there, I am not giving up my career for a dude. Nothing's going to come of it."

Her heart thudded painfully as those words escaped her, but experience was a harsh teacher. No one stuck around for anything but a fling from her, so that was what she had learned to give.

"Fine, but only if you promise to tell them before the wedding if you decide on a second date. No second date, and I will take this to my grave."

Lina licked her palm and stuck it out. Cassie licked her own and took Lina's.

"Spit promise," Cassie said.

"Spit promise," Lina repeated.

"Did you…did you just lick your palms and shake hands?" Wesley's shock was palpable as he entered the kitchen. "Gross."

"Yeah, why do you think I made her do it when we were kids?" Lina chuckled merrily. "Being the big sister lets you get away with shit like that."

Wesley shook his head and grabbed a beer from the fridge. He was an only child. "I'm going to watch football and pretend I never saw anything of the sort. What kind of family am I marrying into?"

"The best kind, of course." Cassie plopped on the couch and turned on the TV. "The kind that loves you without a spit promise."

He laughed and slung his arm around her shoulders. "I guess I can live with that."

His parents were nice. Lina had met them at Granny's funeral, but they weren't what she would call *fun*. Even if Wesley had a sibling, she doubted they would have ever done anything as ridiculous as a spit promise. Well, he had her now. She had to find something worthy of making a spit promise with him. Welcome him to the family in true Schultz fashion.

"How late are the stores open today?" she asked instead.

"Five-ish," Cassie said. "Gonna head out?"

"Yeah. Want to tag along?"

Cassie looked between her and Wes.

"Go on." Wesley shooed them away. "She's only here a few weeks. We have the rest of our lives."

And there was the reason Lina adored Wesley.

Cassie kissed his cheek. "Thanks, hon. I knew I was marrying you for a reason."

She snagged her purse and they were out the door a few minutes later.

"Dunks is on me," Lina said as they walked down the hall. It had been too long since she'd strolled through the cold Boston streets in December nursing her favorite Dunkin' Donuts latte. The perfect holiday activity with her sister.

Chapter 7
Almost a Striptease

Nobody could throw a rock without hitting a good Italian restaurant in the North End, but the chef at Solo Buono used to work at The Old Bell when Dash bought the place. Nichols Entertainment paid for her culinary program and had been rewarded when Shay put his top-tier restaurant in New York on the map. Though she'd struck out on her own a few years later to open this, it was still one of the best damn investments he ever made.

Dash waited outside, people watching. On this mid-December evening, a damp chill hung in the air, its misty presence weighing down those running around bundled up nearly as much as Lina had been the other night. But between calling the North Pole home and elven magic, the cold didn't touch him. It would look weird if he went without some sort of winter outerwear on, though, so Dash donned a tan overcoat and shoved his hands in his pockets.

He checked his watch—nearly seven. Lina should be here any minute.

Dash felt it when she turned the corner, as if somebody had whispered his name and every nerve in his body fired all at once.

Bundled much as she'd been before, she wore a staid navy hat over her curls this time, but her puffy coat and outrageously red scarf were the same.

"Lina!" He waved as she neared.

A beautiful smile answered him, and she quickened her steps, weaving through the crowded streets. She stopped a couple feet in front of him, and for a minute, looked as if she wanted to throw her arms around him. He wished she would. He'd never craved a woman's touch as much as he craved hers right this moment.

Instead, she clasped her hands behind her back and rocked on her heels. "Hi."

"Come on, let's get you out of the cold. You look like you haven't seen a Massachusetts winter in a dog's age."

He held the door, enjoying the view of her swaying hips as she preceded him into the restaurant. They maneuvered through the people waiting for a table until they reached the host stand.

"Dash Nichols for seven o'clock."

The young woman checked the reservation list. "Yes, Mr. Nichols. For two?"

She glanced around, her brows rising when her gaze landed on Lina, who had removed her hat and was trying desperately to control the static waving her curls wildly in the non-existent breeze. Dash found it the most adorable thing ever. He had it bad.

"Yes, thank you."

She grabbed two menus. "Right this way."

Dash gently placed his hand on the small of Lina's back and guided her after the young woman. The thrill of touching her again had his heart pounding and his knees weak. He was beginning to accept the possibility he had found his helpmate. May God have mercy upon his soul. And hers.

The woman led them to a cozy two-top tucked away in a quiet corner, far enough from the flow of traffic to offer a bit of privacy, yet close enough to the kitchen for prompt service. He held out Lina's chair for her and watched as she carefully divested herself of her winter wear.

The gloves came off and were tucked into the hat. Then the scarf. The unraveling took so long, it was almost a striptease. Oh, that was a pretty picture. Lina in just the scarf.

Down, boy.

Finally, she unzipped the puffy coat and peeled it off. She shoved everything into the coat sleeve and hung it on the coatrack near their table.

Dash appreciated the view and suppressed the urge to whistle. Lina wore a simple black dress with a deep V-neck, revealing enough cleavage to give him wank material for years. It ruched across her body to a tie on the left side, emphasizing her generous curves and reminding him of a gift for him to unwrap. Holy mistletoe, how the fuck was he supposed to last through this dinner?

Lina sat and pulled the menu close. Dash hung up his coat and joined her.

"What's good?" She met his gaze over the edge of the menu.

He almost forgot to breathe. In the candlelight, the gold glints in her eyes sparkled and glowed like fires in the hearths at home. She bit her lip when he didn't respond.

"Dash, are you okay? You've hardly said anything. Is something wrong?"

He could do this. He had to do this. Inhaling deeply, he plastered on his panty-dropping smile and soldiered on with the truth.

"No, not at all. You look so amazing you took my breath away."

She flushed but returned a shy smile. "You're teasing me.

That's not nice on a first date."

"I would never. Not on a first date."

She laughed, and the tension drained from her body.

"As far as what's good—everything. I know the chef; she's the best. Do you like Italian?"

"Oh yes, and it's been so long since I've had a good Italian meal. The best I've had recently was the cheese tortellini MRE a couple weeks ago." She made a face that told him her opinion about the field rations.

"So, it's been a while. I didn't know you were in the military."

Lina shook her head. "No, I work for an international aid organization, and the US military sometimes gives us emergency rations in the form of MREs. They're fine, but certainly not North End Italian."

He chuckled and sipped at his water. "No, I suppose not. International aid, huh? What's it like?"

She peered at him over her menu, considering him for a moment, as though judging whether he was worthy of an honest answer. Melancholy settled over her features, but hope shone in her eyes.

"Fulfilling. Sad. Terrifying. Depends on the day, depends on the assignment."

He fought the urge to throw the menu aside and pull her into his arms. This had to be an effect of the helpmate bond. Not that he was a cold-hearted scumbag, but he'd never connected so strongly with a woman this early in the relationship, and he would have to get used to this almost uncontrollable need to comfort her.

The arrival of the server saved him from both embarrassing himself and answering.

"Welcome to Solo Buono. Would you like to hear today's specials?" she asked.

At Dash's nod, she rattled off a veal dish and a pasta dish, but he wasn't paying attention. Instead, Lina's rapt expression sent flutters of something through his gut. He had no idea what it was. All he hoped was to give her a reason to look at him that way. Maybe he, too, could concoct a menu and rattle it off in a perfect Italian accent.

"Those sound terrific, but I would love a simple Bolognese." Lina folded the menu and gave it to the server.

"Of course," the server said and turned to Dash. "For you?"

"I will have the veal, and a bottle of Sassicaia. And a house salad, please."

"Oh, sounds good. I'll take one, too," Lina said.

After the server smiled in acknowledgment, Dash handed over the menu and she disappeared.

"You don't have to impress me." Lina leaned in, eyes wide. "It's the most expensive bottle on the menu."

"But what if I want to impress you?"

"Consider your job done. I've been impressed with you from the first horrible martini."

"Those were handcrafted, artisan chocolate-mint martinis."

"Says the man I puked on."

He laughed loudly and felt truly joyous in a way he hadn't in a while. "Are we going to have a repeat with the wine tonight? Should I change the order?"

She flushed, the rosiness starting between her breasts and spreading up her neck until her cheeks glowed. Despite the strange nature of the conversation, his thoughts still turned to the erotic.

"It's only the sweet stuff. I assume you have the knowledge to not order sweet red wine."

"Does such a thing exist?"

"It's a big world. People are very creative when it comes to alcohol. I'm sure it's out there somewhere. And you're right—those martinis were better than they had a right to be. At least going down."

He smirked, and she ducked her head, suddenly engrossed with the straw in her water.

The sommelier came out with their wine and did the whole cork smelling and tasting the wine ritual. It was always a big show, and Dash never needed a big show. He knew what he liked, and if anything was off, he would send it back. But he enjoyed witnessing Lina's delight. Hands folded under her chin, her rapt expression drank it all in, as though to relive at a later date.

The show over, the sommelier poured them both a glass, and Lina picked up hers. She swirled the wine and sipped slowly, and a pleased smile crossed her lips. Her eyes brightened once more, and he had an inkling of what she might look like if he ever had the chance to shower her body with kisses, explore her luscious curves, and fuck her into senselessness.

"You seem at home here," she said, breaking the trance he was in as he imagined her in throes of passion.

"Hcre?"

"In the world of fine dining. In the restaurant."

Ah, a safe topic. He grabbed hold of it, anything to avoid making a fool of himself. Thankfully, the tablecloth hid his raging erection.

"I've been working in the restaurant business for nearly twenty years. I love it."

"You must. I can't imagine doing any one thing for twenty years. It's why I love international aid. Each assignment is different."

"Oh, I haven't been doing the same job. I mean, I make a damn fine bartender, but I own The Old Bell."

"No!"

"Yep, along with a few other bars in New England, a restaurant in New York, and others in Chicago, Dallas, and

LA."

Her mouth fell open and she blinked slowly. "You're a mogul."

He tried not to preen. Admittedly, he'd had plenty of help from the family fortune. When one's life expectancy was twice that of a human and there was plenty of time to generate interest income, it wasn't hard to amass a significant nest egg. But he went into the restaurant business with more than the money. He had a nose for what concepts would work and what wouldn't, as well as treating his staff and customers well. Not a single penny he invested in his people ever went to waste.

"Well…"

"Dash Nichols, why didn't you warn me you'd be here tonight?" A whirl of white burst from the kitchen and bore down on them.

Dash rose and braced himself. Shay threw herself at him in a bear hug. Their server followed her, carrying the salads.

"I had to hear the gossip from the maître d' that *the* Dash Nichols was gracing us with his presence tonight. With a lovely date in tow, too. What kind of friend are you?"

She swatted Dash on the arm, then turned to Lina and stuck out her hand, not letting him get a word in edgewise.

"Hi, I'm Shay Glazer. This is my restaurant. How on Earth did Dash snag such a gorgeous creature as you?"

Lina shook the hand with a wide smile. "Lina, and he serves a mean chocolate-mint martini."

Shay's brows rose and she pursed her lips as she glared at him. "Really? Who convinced him to make those?"

"My sister is a lawyer and can be extremely persuasive, but I made him regret it," Lina said with a wicked gleam in her eyes.

"Ooh, I like her. I have to get back to the kitchen before the sous chef sets fire to something. He's a bit of a pyro. Please enjoy, and of course your meal is on the house."

"Shay—" Dash started to protest, but there was no stopping her.

"I wouldn't be here if not for you. As long as you're eating in my establishment, you pay for nothing."

Before he could protest once more, Shay left much as she had arrived—a flurry of white chaos.

"She seems…" Lina hesitated as though unsure if she would be insulting Dash's friend.

"A bit much?" He smiled. Shay took over every place she inhabited. It was her way, and part of what made her a fantastic chef. But experiencing it for the first time was a lot to take in.

"A lot much, but she reminds me of my best friend."

He filed away the fact they had similar types of friends. Another hint they might be helpmates.

"Shay would literally give you the shirt off her back. In fact, she works with a homeless shelter, employing some people and making sure all the residents have some good meals. She may comp my meal, but she can't stop me from leaving a generous tip."

"If this is what dating a restaurant mogul is like, I can live with it."

Warm tendrils of delight started low and wound their way through him, touching his heart, his mind, and lodging firmly in his bones. Whatever doubt he had harbored about Lina being his helpmate vanished. Now he just had to figure out how to inform her she was fated to the son of Santa Claus and hope she didn't run away screaming.

CHAPTER 8
SHIPPING AND LOGISTICS

The food was amazing. Even the salad was perfect. And though they hadn't requested it, their server brought out an oversize piece of tiramisu with two forks.

Lina hadn't eaten this well in ages. Work had kept her busy enough she'd left the morning of her flight instead of the night before, so she had no chance to partake of the superb food in Athens. The last time she'd visited Boston was for her grandmother's funeral a year and a half ago. Everything had tasted like sawdust, no matter where they'd found it. And though she never went hungry, meals in the refugee camp were not this fancy and fresh. They kept it simple, eating with the people they served when possible and only occasionally making the trip to the capital.

But this, this was near heaven. And the company…it had been even longer since she'd enjoyed herself with a man this much. She didn't want the night to end.

Before long, though, the tiramisu was gone, her wine glass was empty, and the hour grew late. The restaurant was emptying, and the staff rushed a little less than they had before.

Dash hadn't once looked at the expensive watch on his wrist.

He kept her talking about her work, her sister, the wedding, but he hadn't divulged too much about himself.

"What about you?" Lina couldn't let tonight go, not yet. "What's your family like?"

His mouth twisted into a wry grin. "We're tight, but my dad's a little disappointed I'm not very involved in the family business."

"What is the family business?" If she kept him talking, she might muster the courage to take him someplace more private. Her sister's condo was out.

Dash pressed his lips together, and his eyes sparkled. She could lose herself in those baby blues.

"Shipping and logistics," he said. "I'll eventually have to take over, at least as a figurehead, but Dad's still hale and hearty. Nobody's pushing him out until he's good and ready."

International aid relied heavily on quickly transporting equipment, supplies, and people from one part of the world to another, and Lina had developed many contacts in shipping and logistics. She might have to look up the company, discover if her organization had any connection with Dash's family business. But later. Digging deep before they were officially dating would be creepy.

"Any siblings?"

"A younger sister."

"Ugh, they're the worst." Not really, not once they both became adults. But there were a few years as teenagers where Lina was unsure which of them would make it out alive.

"Yes, they are. I love Joy to death, and she should take over the business once Dad retires, not me, but she's the most annoying person on the planet."

"Oh, you're wrong there. Cassie is the most annoying person on the planet."

A few minutes of comparing little sister horror stories later, and neither of them made a move to leave. She finally said something once she noticed they were the last customers in the place.

"It's late, and these people need to get home."

He blinked as though coming out of a trance. "Oh, yeah. That would not be a kind thing to do."

He pulled out his wallet and dropped a few hundred-dollar bills on the table. There would be no check, but the cash should pay for the meal, the wine, and a hefty tip. Though her family had never wanted for anything, dropping several hundred dollars on a meal was a rarity. In fact, she doubted it had ever happened outside of large family gatherings for important events like graduations and funerals.

Lina used to be uneasy around such largesse, but since fundraising was also a big part of her job, she'd become at least a little used to it. Some of their wealthy supporters often hosted $500-plate dinners. But she had only had someone spend that much money on dinner with her once before, a wealthy donor who convinced her to go on a date. He'd been nice enough, but she was firm in her desire to continue her career, and he hadn't called again.

She stood and grabbed her coat, pulling the hat, scarf, and gloves from the sleeve.

"Thank you, Dash. I had a wonderful evening."

"Trust me, the pleasure was all mine. Let me walk you to the T. Or would you prefer a rideshare?"

"The T is fine."

Once again, his hand found the small of her back. With most other men in her past, it had felt as though they were trying to guide her where they wanted her. But with Dash, it made her feel safe, and more like he was reassuring himself she was real.

He was nearly everything she was looking for. Kind and confident, with strong family ties, and breathtakingly gorgeous.

He was easy to talk to, and his smile warmed her to her core. And it was interesting they both had strong friendships with over-the-top women.

They walked out into the frosty December night and straight to the nearest station. Before she ducked in, she turned to say goodbye. The streetlight glinted in his eyes, and there was a fire in them calling her name. She couldn't resist.

Lina rose on her tiptoes and pressed her lips to his. Dash wrapped his arms around her and drew her close with a low groan of pleasure. She melted into him, and he deepened the kiss, teasing her lips with his tongue. His beard scratched against her in a pleasurable juxtaposition to the softness of his lips. He tasted of tiramisu, creamy coffee and amaretto, wine, and something crisp and clean, like mint but not.

Dash broke away long before Lina was ready to let him go. She reached out to him, but he clasped her gloved hand and held it next to his face.

"I want nothing more than to take you home and kiss you all night long, among other things." His rough voice sent a shiver of unadulterated lust down her spine to nestle in her core. The warmth of it pooled between her legs.

"Why don't you?" she asked before she could stop herself. But she would say yes. This man made her throw caution to the wind.

He chuckled. "You need to be sure, and you're not there yet."

"But you are?"

"Oh yes, I'm sure. I also don't want you to regret anything we do. Anything. I'm a patient man."

"What if I'm not a patient woman?"

He pulled her hand to his lips and kissed it through the glove. She'd never been so frustrated over wearing gloves in December as she was at that moment.

"All the better, but let's go on at least one more date."

"Playing the gentleman?"

"I'm no gentleman, and I look forward to proving it to you."

"Me, too."

And he kissed her again, pulling her in tight and claiming her mouth. She let him—no, she encouraged him. Little mewling sounds escaped her, and despite the cold, she wished for more skin. His, hers, it didn't matter, just more. Their tongues tangled and their breaths came hot and fast, surrounding them in clouds of their own pleasure.

"Get a room," someone muttered as they passed into the station.

Once again, Dash broke away first, a lascivious grin painted on his lips. "I will."

"Not if I do first."

"Goodnight, Lina." Dash stepped back, but it seemed to pain him. "I'll call in the morning."

"You better."

She turned away before she decided to climb him like a cat climbed a Christmas tree. Lina did not understand these extreme reactions, but she couldn't deny he fulfilled her fantasies in a way she would be a fool to turn down.

His laugh followed her into the station, a hearty ho, ho, ho. Weirdo.

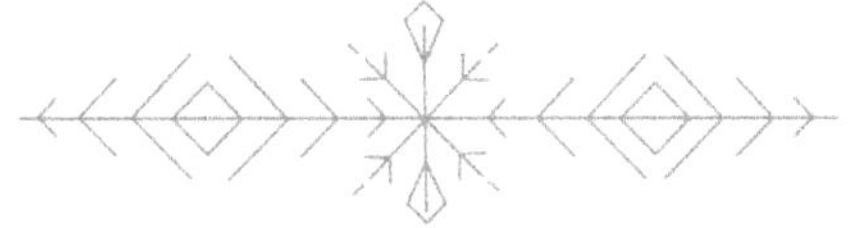

CHAPTER 9
EXACTLY FIVE MINUTES

He didn't wait until morning. Dash didn't even wait until she got home. He waited exactly five minutes, and every last one was excruciating.

"I thought you said you'd call in the morning." Her mellifluous voice both soothed and excited him. Yep, he was royally screwed.

It wasn't only the helpmate bond, though. Nor was it her gorgeous, curvaceous figure. It might be the important work she was doing. Or how she poked fun at her little sister with a fierce love shining in her eyes. Or the longing in her expression after he kissed her.

"What, no hello?"

"Hello, Dash." The smile in her voice carried through the echoey connection. "Why are you calling? Did I leave something in the restaurant?"

"No, nothing like that. I just didn't want you to be alone on the T. There are strange people this time of night."

"Tell me about it."

His pulse raced and his mind flipped through various scenarios she could be facing this very moment. He halted mid-step and fished in his pocket for the key. Didn't matter if he blew the family secret sky high—if Lina was in trouble, he would ride to her rescue.

"This one dude, he called me five minutes after we said goodnight."

Pure deadpan. So dry, it would be at home in the Mojave. He loved it. He loved—

Fuuuck. Nope, not going there tonight. He would not declare his undying love after the first date. Even with the helpmate bond, could he truly be in love with somebody after only one date, as amazing as it was? Sadly, the answer was probably yes, at least in this case. She was everything he'd been looking for, funny, smart, compassionate. Though he might be bound by fate to this woman, he wasn't going to scare her away yet, not for all the hot cocoa in the world. He would let the nine reindeer and his father do that.

"Ha, ha, ha," he said.

"Don't you mean, ho, ho, ho? 'Tis the season."

"You're a riot. Really."

The smile wouldn't leave his face. He must look like some serial killer, walking down the street on a frigid night with this ridiculous grin, talking on the phone. Dash didn't give a polar bear's ass. Let them stare. For the first time in a long time, he was truly happy.

"I know. I consistently win the annual talent show with my jokes."

"You do?"

"No, no one gets my sense of humor. Except my sister. And, apparently, you."

And if that didn't scream helpmate, nothing did. He craved only to bask in her presence until she kicked him out into the snow. Instead, he was talking with her on the phone as he tried to find a suitable door, and she tried to make her way home.

"Tell me again, why aren't you coming home with me?" It slipped out before his brain could warn him away.

"Because you didn't ask."

"Then invite me to your place."

"A, I don't invite strange men back to my place. And B, my place is technically halfway around the world. I'm staying with my sister and her fiancé, and…yikes, that's a line I don't want to cross."

Oh yeah, he forgot. Eventually, she would return to her assignment in Greece. Of course, distance meant nothing to an elf with an enchanted key that could open a door to anywhere in the world. How else were all the Christmas presents distributed? The sleigh and reindeer were PR at this point, a healthy distraction while the rest of the North Pole staff slipped in and out of homes all around the world.

But he was an elf, and many humans reacted poorly to learning they weren't the only sentient species on the planet. He doubted Lina would be one of those, but still, elves, Santa, magic—they could be hard pills to swallow. This was future Dash's problem. Present Dash need only be concerned with convincing her to take the next step.

He chuckled and darted down an alley. Yes, this door would work.

"I am not a strange man. You know my name and where I work. I told you my sister's name, and about the family business. What else do you need to know?"

He leaned against the wall and wondered what she was doing. Was she watching the stops flicker by? Was she trying to avoid eye contact with a real stranger? Was she merely humoring him?

"Hmm," Lina said. "What's your favorite color?"

"Whatever color you're wearing."

She giggled, and his cock twitched. From a simple giggle, lord help him.

"Favorite book?"

"Trick question. Anybody who can name just one book doesn't read enough." He imagined her cradling the phone next to her ear, then imagined it was his palm and bit back a grunt of frustration.

"Fine, favorite book this year?"

"The latest by Michael Connelly."

"Oh, say it ain't so."

"What can I say? I like a good mystery thriller I can pick up at any airport or grocery store." Business kept him busy, but he enjoyed escaping for a bit every once in a while. "How about you?"

"Have you heard of Emily Henry?"

"No…but it sounds like I might have a new author to check out."

"You should," she said with her excitement palpable through the phone. Then a thoughtful pause. "Well, maybe not."

"If you like it, it's worth trying. We don't have to read the same books to date."

A beat of silence. He checked to make sure the call hadn't dropped.

"I know." A pensive sort of pause, then she sighed. "You understand I have to go back right after New Year's."

"Yes, but that doesn't mean I can't enjoy the time you're here." He planned to make her realize distance wasn't an issue. Not for the son of Santa.

"Okay. I won't give up my work. It might be heartbreaking, but it's important, and there aren't enough people willing to do it." There was warm iron in her words. She truly cared about what she was doing, the people she helped. Good for her.

And he would do everything in his power to support her.

"I understand, and I would never ask you to."

"As long as we're clear. Listen, I'm almost to my stop. Is there anything else?"

"What are you doing for lunch tomorrow?" He wanted to see her again now, but tomorrow would do, barely.

"Um, let me check my calendar. Hmm, nope, sorry, meeting with the mayor. How about a week from Tuesday?"

"You're teasing me. That's not nice on a first date."

She laughed, a rich, warm blanket he could wrap around himself forever. Soon enough, he would have his forever. First, he needed to convince Lina he was hers.

"Where do you want to meet?"

The swish of the doors of the T opening and the echoey sounds of people in a subway station floated from her end of the call.

"Fenway," he said firmly, leaving no room to argue. "There's a great lunch spot near there. Meet you at the T station at noon."

"Great. See you tomorrow."

Dash couldn't bring himself to end the call. Apparently, she couldn't either. The line stayed open, the echoes of her footsteps his only company.

"Lina?"

"Yes?"

"You're supposed to hang up."

"No, *you're* supposed to hang up."

"On three?"

A playfully exasperated huff sent tingles along every nerve in his body.

"Fine. One," she said.

"Two."

"Three."

He made himself hit the button. No need to make an even bigger fool of himself tonight. He had his entire life to do so.

Dash pulled the special key out of his pocket and turned the magical lock that appeared. He stepped into his real world. The one where he would have to explain to his parents he was falling in love with a human. Again. But this time, the human was his helpmate.

CHAPTER 10
LET THE FUTURE SORT ITSELF OUT

Cassie ambushed Lina the moment she walked into the apartment.

Waiting with two glasses of wine, her sister bounced on her toes like a five-year-old who needed to visit the little girl's room right the hell now. Cassie thrust a glass at Lina before she had a chance to remove her gloves, let alone her hat and coat. Wesley was nowhere to be seen.

"Spill," Cassie ordered before taking a sip of the wine.

"Where's Wes?"

"Asleep. He's got a big meeting first thing."

"Aren't you working?" Lina put the glass on the entry table and shucked her outerwear.

"Yes, but I do not have a big meeting first thing. And you'd be amazed how often people give a bride-to-be some slack when the wedding is only two weeks away."

Cassie snagged Lina's arm and pulled her to the living room as soon as her wine glass was back in her hand. Lina dropped onto the couch and tucked her legs under her. Cassie mirrored her position, but her face grew serious.

"Are you going to make me go all courtroom lawyer on you,

or are you going to make it easy on yourself and tell me the whole truth and nothing but the truth?"

Lina took a sip of her wine, deciding what to say.

"Can you even handle the truth?" she finally said with a small smile.

"Fine, Jack, tell me pretty little lies so I can live vicariously through you. I'm getting hitched, and God willing, I will have no more first dates, good or bad."

Lina spilled, but not because of her sister's pitiful pleas. Wes treated Cassie like a queen, and they still had a strong spark, even after several years. Lina spilled her guts because she couldn't believe it was real. Hottie McBartender liked her. Flirted with her. Hadn't been thrown off by her job. And if the bulge in his jeans when they'd kissed was any indication, would like nothing better than to fuck her into next Sunday.

"Well, you're very fuckable," Cassie said after Lina finished.

"Ew. That's just…no. We're sisters, not friends."

"We can be both."

"Yeah, but not when it comes to sexy stuff."

"Fine. I withdraw the comment. You, Carolina Schultz, are a beautiful, desirable woman any man would be lucky to date. And as long as he treats you right, I am ecstatic you found someone who might appreciate you."

Being in a remote part of the world, often too busy coping with disasters both natural and manmade, left little time or opportunity to date. The few occasions she tried to build a real relationship, the guy she was dating insisted she quit her job. It wasn't a job, it wasn't even a career. It was a calling. As she'd told Dash, her work was important, more important than any previous relationship. It meant a lot he understood.

At least, he said he understood. So had a few others, and when push came to shove, they'd bailed, breaking her heart. Could she risk that again?

"I'm going back two days after the wedding. Then what?"

Cassie patted her knee. "You worry too much about 'then what.' Live in the moment. Take Hottie McBartender for the gift he is and let the future sort itself out."

"But—"

"No buts unless you're talking about Dash. I wouldn't mind talking about his butt."

Lina threw a pillow and missed. On purpose, of course. "What would your fiancé say if he heard you talking about another man like that?"

"I'm engaged, not dead. I can admire the occasional firm ass."

Peals of giggles filled the living room. So much better than her last visit. Lina had missed this, had missed Cassie. Sure, her work was rewarding—beyond rewarding. But it didn't leave the space she wished for her family and friends. Speaking of which…

"I'm meeting Tiên for a movie tomorrow night," Lina said.

"Date-date and friend-date on the same day. Are you finally turning into a social butterfly at the ripe old age of thirty-two?"

"Who knows? Give me another decade and I'll start going to clubs like some kind of extrovert."

They finished their wine, and Cassie slipped off to bed. Lina washed the glasses and shuffled to the guest room.

She had decidedly erotic dreams that night featuring one Mr. Dash Nichols with the twinkling blue eyes, yet she woke more well-rested than she'd been in weeks.

The condo was quiet with both Cassie and Wes off to work, but she loaded a pod into the fancy coffee machine and poured a bowl of cereal. Lunch near Fenway would be a casual affair, so leggings and a sweater should be fine. But she needed to do her hair and makeup.

She stepped off the T a few minutes before noon and walked

into the cold December sunshine. And there he was, waiting for her. Lina was always early, but still he beat her.

His smile when he spotted her sent warmth to her heart and a pool of heat to her core. It wasn't even his super sexy smile, and she was already wet for him. Damn, what would her reaction be when he *was* trying to get in her pants?

"Lina!"

His melodious baritone sent shivers of anticipation through her body. He encircled her with his brawny arms and gently kissed her in a very appropriate way for a second date. Fuck appropriate.

Lina opened for him and flicked her tongue against his lower lip. His low growl set her blood thrumming with lust. She needed to figure out a way to tempt him into her bed soon. Or finagle her way into his. Whatever would work.

Dash pulled away and rested his forehead against hers. "That wasn't fair. Now, how am I going to concentrate on lunch?"

"Not my problem."

"I could make it your problem."

"Please do."

He groaned and stepped back. "I don't want you to think I only want in your pants."

"I don't mind," she purred, and closed the distance once more, sliding her hand around to cup his ass. "I wore the stretchy kind that are easy to take off."

Another rumble deep in his chest issued forth as he snaked an athletic arm around her waist and lowered his mouth to hers. She fit just right into his hard body, as if he'd been made for her. Even through all the layers between them, his muscles flexed under her touch. And the bulge she noticed last night pressed against her, rock hard and ready for a good time. What Lina wouldn't give for a bit of privacy…

Dash came up for air, panting as if he'd run a mile. "Lina,

you're killing me."

She smiled, and it must have been her best, most sultry one, because Dash flushed like a teenager.

"Wouldn't that put me on Santa's naughty list? There must be much better ways to get on the list than being the cause of your death."

He kissed her again, quick and fierce, barely enough to satisfy, but more than enough to promise.

"Come on, we can negotiate what comes next over the lunch I promised you. A Nichols always keeps their promise."

He tugged her down the street. What on Earth had gotten into her? It wasn't like her to flirt so outrageously, but it came so easy when she was with Dash.

Lina was so lost in thought, it took her a moment to realize they'd reached their destination. Dash opened the door to a little hole-in-the-wall diner. The salty scent of bacon brought her back to reality, and her mouth watered. He led her to a booth in the far corner of the restaurant.

"Is this one of the places you own?" Lina wriggled into the booth and pulled off her gloves.

Dash slid into the small two-person booth opposite her. He clasped her hands in his large, warm ones. Which was a bit odd, considering they'd come in from the cold and he hadn't been wearing gloves.

"No, just been coming here for years. Do you trust me?"

Her eyes narrowed and her lips twisted in a funny little half smile. "Depends on what you're asking me to trust you with."

"Let me see if I can order the perfect meal for you."

Lina generally didn't appreciate her dates ordering for her, in part because of her past issues with accepting herself as she was. Mostly, it stunk of old-fashioned bullshit. But Dash was in the restaurant industry and had great taste, if dinner last night was any sign.

"Why?" She folded her hands neatly on the table, a gesture she'd picked up from her father when he questioned her motives as a teen.

"It's a game I play to make the shifts pass quicker. What would this person's perfect meal be? Are you a gambler?"

Lina enjoyed a good bet, and she was curious what he might put on the table. "Okay, what if you get it wrong?"

"If I get it wrong, you pick our next activity."

"Anything?"

Heat flared in his eyes, and an answering flame burned bright in her chest.

"Anything," he said, voice rough. "But if I get it right, I pick."

It was a win-win situation to Lina. "Deal."

He smiled like a cat that had knocked all the ornaments off the Christmas tree. "You wait here."

Dash slid out of the booth and walked to the counter. Cassie was right—he had an incredible ass. She could watch it for days and never grow bored. The server took the order and gave it to the kitchen, and Dash returned.

He held her hands again. "So tell me about your missing hat."

Lina tensed in her seat, but he did not let go.

"I'm sorry, is it a sore subject?" he asked.

"No, I didn't expect you to remember."

"Why wouldn't I? It was obviously important to you, and you were upset. And, not for nothing, it's what brought you back to me."

She couldn't help the teasing smile his comment brought forth. "You were already pining for me?"

"Oh yes. If you had paid rather than a bridesmaid, I would have tracked you down using the receipt."

"Isn't that illegal?"

"Probably. Would you have turned me in?" He gave her puppy-dog eyes with an undercurrent of smolder. Holy crap, he gave good smolder.

"Probably not."

His rich laugh filled the air, and her own chuckle intertwined beautifully with it.

"So, the hat?"

"Granny made it for me in high school. It was her last project before her sight got too bad to knit anymore."

"Is that why…"

"It has horrendous colors?"

"I was trying to think of a more polite way of saying that, but yes."

"No. The colors were my choice."

He blinked in surprise. "Your choice?"

"As the wicked smart kid who was too introverted to hang out with the other weirdos at school, I didn't fit in. I could change everything about myself to conform, or I could lean into the weird."

His thumb gently rubbed her knuckles. It was meant to be a comforting gesture, and she was comforted. But she was also turned on. Big time. This man was going to be her undoing, and she couldn't wait. Please, let him get the order wrong.

"You leaned in."

"You bet your ass."

He beamed at this in amusement, but there was also a hint of pride.

"I asked Granny to make me the ugliest hat she could. I swear that's how my best friend Tiên found me. Together, we made a few equally odd friends, and we survived long enough to graduate and go to college, where we finally found our people and flourished."

"Good for you, and good for them. So the hat was a talisman."

She'd never thought of it that way before, but it was both a symbol of her acceptance of herself and a tangible symbol of someone's love for her, just as she was.

"Yes."

"I guess I'm going to have to scour the greater Boston area to find it for you."

Her heart leaped. It was an impossible task, but his willingness to offer touched her soul. And made her want to climb him even more. What was it with this guy?

"You know that's impossible, right?"

He finally let go of her and interlaced his fingers, stretching his arms overhead, then side to side. "Impossible is my middle name."

She was still chuckling when the server came with their food.

"Okay, who had the bacon cheeseburger?" the young man asked.

Dash gestured briefly. "That would be me."

The server set a basket filled with fries and an appropriately sized cheeseburger. Neither too big nor too small. Then he set a basket in front of Lina. Instead of fries, there were tots. Nestled into the abundance of fried potatoes was a triple-decker BLT on toasted bread.

"And who gets the chocolate frappe?" The server's gaze darted between them.

"Me again," Dash said with a wide grin.

"This must be yours, miss."

He set a glass filled to the brim with strawberry frappe, topped with a healthy helping of whipped cream, and instead of a cherry, it had a chocolate-covered strawberry on top.

"Enjoy," he said before returning to the counter.

"Well?" Dash tapped his fingers on the table in an impatient rhythm.

"The chocolate-covered strawberry is a nice touch. What kind of bread?"

An impish smile tilted up the corners of his full lips. Damn, she wanted to kiss him.

"Sourdough. And I ordered extra tomato."

Lina slid the glass and basket to the side, and his face fell. Then she stood, leaned over the table, and gave into the urge to kiss him as though her life depended on it.

CHAPTER 11
WITH A BOW AND EVERYTHING

Dash drank her up like a man too long in the desert. She hadn't eaten anything yet and still tasted of toothpaste. Her lips were soft against his, and he craved more. So much more.

She broke away with a sexy hum and pulled her meal in front of her.

"I guess this means I won," he said with a smirk.

"Don't get cocky. You have no idea what you're giving up."

Her face brightened as she took a sip of her milkshake—no, it was a frappe in New England. They made the best strawberry frappe in Massachusetts here. The owner was an elf, a distant cousin, if he remembered correctly.

"I'm not giving up anything. You may not have heard, but the anticipation is part of the gift."

"Oh, are you saying you're some sort of gift?"

"Do you want me to be? I can wrap myself nicely, with a bow and everything."

She choked a little on her drink. Only her quick action to cover her mouth and nose with a napkin saved him from a shower of strawberry frappe. Which, to be honest, would be a lot better than chocolate-mint vomit.

"You realize how close you came to being covered in my spit again, don't you?" she said once she gained control over herself.

He widened his smirk, his mind happily dancing right into the gutter. Lina flushed and suddenly turned her attention to her BLT. She took a bite and made appreciative noises. Noises he was glad to be the cause of, and ones he would very much like to cause in a much more direct way. Preferably without clothes on.

They ate in silence for a few moments, both recovering their composure.

"So, what's the plan?" she asked, most of her tots and half her sandwich gone.

What *was* the plan? He yearned for nothing other than to coax her into his bed as soon as possible. Worship her with his hands, his tongue, his cock. But he lived with his parents. And his sister. He needed a bit of time to plan, perhaps book a hotel room. Or convince his family to leave him alone for one night—a week before Christmas.

"Give me your phone," he said.

Lina unlocked it and handed it over. He opened the notes app and typed in an address to a friend's place. It would do as a way station. He could use the basement door to take her to his home, assuming she was onboard with his plan.

"I have a confession." He slid the phone back to her. "I live with my parents."

She sipped her frappe again. "No judgment from me. I'm crashing with my sister."

"It's a big place, and I have a private entrance. I have a shift at the bar, or otherwise we'd be doing this tonight. Unless I text you, meet me at that address tomorrow at eight p.m. No expectations, okay, no pressure, but I'd like to spend the night with you. Bring an overnight bag if you want. Whether we do anything other than talk is entirely up to you."

Lina bit her lip and her knuckles whitened as she gripped the phone. Dash steeled himself for rejection.

"I'd like that too, Dash. But I have to fly back to Greece two days after my sister's wedding. Whatever this is, it's over then."

Dash suppressed a smile. With his special key and a little elven magic, distance was nothing to the son of Santa. He could make it work, but first he had to tell her the whole truth. The last time he tried to tell a human about elves, magic, and the North Pole, it was a shit show. Victoria was the perfect girlfriend until he broke her sanity with the truth. What would happen when he told Lina?

There was no way he would risk it in a diner near Fenway Park. It would be much better to show her the aurora borealis and the workshop. It was the only way she would believe him.

"I can live with that."

Her grip on the phone relaxed, and a small smile replaced the anxious sheen. "Okay."

"Okay?"

She rolled her eyes. "I will meet you at this address tomorrow at eight."

He lifted her hand to his lips and pressed a kiss to her knuckles. "Excellent."

They finished their meals, and Lina insisted on paying. It wasn't worth his time to argue. He would collect on the debt in another way. The fantasy of it had him hard, and he was grateful the overcoat was long enough to hide the evidence of his desire.

He walked her to the T station and kissed her. She melted into him, tasting of strawberries and something just her, a little like cinnamon and cayenne. All he wanted to do was keep kissing her, her soft body nestled into him, and know she was his.

But she wasn't, not yet. Lina couldn't be his until he told her the truth. And even then…the idea the supernatural world was real might be a little hard to swallow. That he wasn't human might be harder. And the fact he would eventually inherit the mantle of Santa Claus might be beyond belief.

Dash let her go. "Thank you for lunch, Lina. I look forward to tomorrow."

Her gloved thumb grazed her bottom lip, her cheeks all rosy, and her breaths made quick puffs of vapor in the cold air.

"Yes, tomorrow."

She ducked into the station, but spared him a glance over her shoulder, a promise burning in her gaze.

Dash found a quiet street and a locked door. He pulled the magic key from his pocket and went home. Somebody had cleaned his room. His bed was made, his clothes hung in the closet, and the sharp scent of cleaner irritated his nose. At least it would be gone by the time Lina arrived tomorrow.

He shed his jacket, throwing it over the chair in the corner, and made his way to the kitchen. He needed a beer and some quiet to brood. Snagging a Winter Lager from the fridge, he took it to the boardroom and the window seat his grandmother had made. Dash leaned against the wall, put his feet on the cushion with his knees up. So close to the winter solstice, all he could do was stare into the infinite dark of the arctic.

How was he going to explain Lina to his parents? How was he going to explain his parents to Lina? Though flings between elves and humans were common, in the end, most elves settled down with other elves. It was too difficult to create a life when you had to lie about where you lived and hide who you really were from the in-laws.

His unoccupied hand went to his ears, the only physical tell he wasn't human. He still wore the glamour, but it only hid the ears; it didn't change them. Toying with the delicate points, Dash tried to imagine what Lina's reaction would be when he told her the truth. Would she believe in magic or would she deem him delusional?

Victoria had refused to believe at first. When he dropped the glamour and showed her the key and how it worked, she rambled on about demons and hallucinations. She became so obsessed with elves and magic, she could no longer think of anything else, begging him constantly to show his ears and take her places using the key.

She had rambled to the wrong person, and rumors of her mental instability made the rounds through their friend group. So he'd called in the big guns—Cricket was a whiz with potions—and a laced mug of mulled wine later, Victoria remembered nothing about the North Pole, Santa, flying reindeer, or much about Dash himself. Just a nice boy she had dated in college whose parents didn't like her.

But Victoria hadn't been his helpmate. Lina was—he would stake his life on it. Hell, he was staking his life on it, his life as he knew it.

"A candy cane for your thoughts." His mother's voice echoed in the otherwise empty room, bouncing off all the glass and hard surfaces.

"Hi, Mom." He should have known. Katja Nichols had an uncanny sense for when her children might need comfort, advice, or company.

She snagged one of the incongruous corporate-looking wheeled desk chairs and slid it across the floor next to him. Sitting, she propped her feet next to his on the cushioned seat.

"You've been MIA lately, and my mommy-sense is tingling."

He would never take her to a Spider-Man movie again. Mommy-sense, for chrissakes.

"The Christmas season is a busy time of year in the restaurant business. You know that—I've been doing this for almost twenty years."

She gave him a tight smile. "Did you forget I'm a living lie detector?"

No, he hadn't. That's why he told her a truth. Not the whole truth, but it was true.

"I'm not sixteen anymore. I've got this."

"Uh-huh. Then why are you drinking a beer in the boardroom? You only come in here when we make you or you have something major to work out."

He wiped a hand down his face. Not only did his mother have this second sense, but she was damned observant, too. "Has anybody ever told you you're too nosy?"

Her smile was genuine this time. "Nearly every day and twice on Christmas."

Dash couldn't help it—he chuckled. She patted his shoulder.

"I'm a good listener, Dash, and I've been to more reindeer roundups than I can count. What's on your mind?"

"There's a woman. I'm almost positive she's my helpmate."

A strange expression crossed his mother's face, a grimace that wanted to be a smile but was duking it out with a serious, take-no-prisoners stoic facade. The facade won.

"Oh?"

Her tone was all too calm. When any other elf declared they'd found their helpmate, it was next to impossible to stop his mother from throwing a party or at least popping some bubbly. He appreciated the effort.

When he didn't respond to the subtle prompt, she gave him a much more obvious one.

"So, what's the problem?"

Lina was kind, funny, gorgeous, and already dedicated to doing good in the world. She would fit right in, except for one tiny fact.

"She's human."

Dash had to give his mother credit. There was no flinch, no

gasp, not even any sort of change to her expression.

"Ah, yes, that's a bit of a sticky candy cane, isn't it?"

"It did not go well last time."

"To be fair, Victoria wasn't your helpmate."

True, but it had been messy.

"How did you know it was Dad?"

Her expression softened into wistful remembering. She squeezed his arm.

"There was this instant spark. I couldn't get him out of my head, no matter what I did. The world seemed brighter when he was near and sadder when he wasn't. And after our first kiss, I just knew. He told me later he felt the same."

He was so fucked. Everything his mother said was what he experienced around Lina.

"Mom." It was a plea, though he wasn't sure what for.

She scooted the chair closer, put an arm around his shoulder, and drew him in for a hug.

"It's going to be okay, Dash. I promise. I can't wait to meet her."

He leaned into her and for a moment felt like a teenager again, still trying to figure out the world and his place in it. He was thirty-nine, for pity's sake, successful by any measure, and had his pick of any woman he desired, elf or human. But Lina's arrival had sent him spiraling. He wanted her, needed her, because of some magical bond nobody claimed to understand. From all evidence, she was a good person, and she fulfilled every fantasy about a woman he'd ever had.

Not only was she gorgeous, but he could get lost in her Christmassy eyes for hours. Her laugh made him want to laugh, too. She fought the good fight, bringing hope where little was found.

What if their budding relationship fizzled worse than Rudolph IV's nose in 1985? What if she rejected him? What if she *wanted* to forget him?

He could back out. Not show up tomorrow. Call her and say he was having second thoughts. Break it off before it hurt too much.

But the problem was the mere notion of never seeing her again hurt worse than anything he'd ever experienced. It was already too late. His only choice was to try. The reward would be great, but he didn't dare imagine what would happen if he failed.

Dash pulled away from his mother. "Thanks, I needed that."

"Any time. I didn't stop being your mom when you turned eighteen. I'm still here, ready to give whatever advice you still need. Or a hug."

She stood and pushed the squeaky chair back to the table.

"Hey, Mom, can I ask a small favor?"

"Sure."

"Can you keep Dad and Joy occupied tomorrow night?"

His mother winked at him and laid a finger on the side of her nose. "I got it covered. Have fun!"

Chapter 12
Where the Fuck Is Your Hat?

Tiên wrapped her in a bear hug so tight Lina was afraid she had bruised a rib.

"It's been way too long, you world-traveling bitch," Tiên said. "Let me look at you."

She snagged Lina's arm and dragged her into the movie theater lobby. Once under the lights, Tiên snatched the hat from her head and unwound the scarf.

"Hey!" Lina attempted to protest, though it would do no good.

Tiên had few boundaries, especially with her. They were as close as sisters, maybe closer. She would tell Tiên all her naughty fantasies about Dash.

Tiên peered at her, pursing her lips in concentration. "At least you're not pasty, and I do believe you have a man in your life, but Carolina, my dear, where the fuck is your hat?"

She waved at the plain navy hat Lina had borrowed from Cassidy. Lina sniffed and her shoulders dropped.

"Lost it."

"You lost your granny hat? Oh, babe, I'm sorry."

Tiên pulled her in for another hug, this one gentle. Her BFF from high school was the only person besides Cassie who understood the importance of her hat. And, surprisingly, Dash. She had never felt so seen by a person she'd known for a few days, which both scared her and made her want to take the next step all the more.

"Thanks."

"Okay, this calls for something stronger than popcorn and soda. There's a bar across the street. I can catch Chris Evans on screen later, but I need to know the story behind the hat. And the man."

Once again, Tiên tugged her along, this time out the doors and across the street to a pleasant-looking bar, Christmas lights all twinkling, and a real evergreen wreath on the door. There was a small, unoccupied table in a corner, and they sat.

"How do you do that?" Lina asked as the server approached.

"Do what?"

"Know when I have a man in my life?"

"What'll it be, ladies?" Their server was a handsome man who only had eyes for Tiên. Which was typical, and fine by Lina. She only had eyes for Dash at the moment.

"A rum and coke and a Winter Lager, if you please," Tiên answered with a sweet smile. Though Lina hated when men ordered for her, Tiên had a free pass and knew Lina's favorite drink this time of year.

Her smile had fooled Lina when they first met. Second month of high school, and Tiên had plopped beside Lina with her lunch box and the sweetest smile.

"Hey, you're Carolina, right? We have English third period."

Tiên, with her straight black hair and expressive brown eyes, cute with the right amount of curves, was usually the type who sat next to Lina to tease her. Or occasionally because they wanted a favor from her, like help with homework or to trade partners for class projects.

Lina was wary but answered anyway. "Yeah, but only my mom calls me

Carolina. It's just Lina."

"Well, just Lina, I'm Tiên. I moved here from New Jersey, and you look like the kind of person worth knowing."

Lina sniffed. So teasing it was. At least that was more honest than being nice just to wheedle something out of her. "Did Heather send you?"

Tiên gave her a once over and intuitively grasped the situation. "I'm not like those losers, I swear. You're smart and funny, and you remind me of my favorite cousin. I want to be friends with someone who can pull off a hat like yours."

Her hand rose to the hat Granny had made for her, with various-sized stripes in random colors, and a big, bright green pom on top. Lina nodded and Tiên joined her.

And she hadn't regretted it one day. Not even when her friend was grilling her on the new guy in her life, as she was now.

"So, dealer's choice." Tiên fiddled with the sugar packets. "You want to talk about the hat or the guy?"

"Neither."

"Wedding it is! Excellent." Tiên rubbed her hands together. "How was the bachelorette party?"

Lina forced down a groan. The bachelorette party led directly to Dash.

"It was fine. I barely made it, and everyone was more than half drunk when I showed up."

"That's all I get? What about the strippers?"

"What strippers? This is Cassie we're talking about. She may flirt a good game, but you and I both know she would never hire strippers."

Tiên shoved her shoulder. "Thus why the maid of honor is supposed to do it, chucklehead."

"I was halfway around the world with barely any internet and no cell service. And how would it have looked using a computer owned by an international aid organization to order a stripper for my little sister?"

"You email the details to your BFF, of course. Sheesh, didn't I teach you anything in high school?"

Lina finally glanced at Tiên, who had the most put-upon expression. She couldn't keep it in anymore and broke into pealing giggles that had their server looking at them strangely when he returned with their drinks.

"Thanks." Tiên wiped tears from her cheeks.

"Everything okay?" he asked.

"Yeah, old friends, long time, you know how it is."

He smiled, but it didn't reach his eyes. He shook his head as he left. Dash would've understood.

"I wouldn't waste my time on that guy, Tiên." Lina raised her glass and toasted her friend.

"Wasn't planning on it. Good looker, but a little lacking in the sense of humor department."

They talked about everything except Lina's hat and Dash. She waited for it, though, knowing it would come. They covered the year and a half since Granny's funeral. Tiên's latest group of high school sophomores, her parents' recent cruise, her brother's new baby. Lina's ongoing assignment and the wedding plans. Tiên finally circled back.

"So, hat or guy?" Tiên asked, on her third rum and coke.

Lina had stopped after two drinks. Though beer wasn't going to send her praying to the porcelain god, she didn't drink often and had a low tolerance.

"Well, they're kind of related."

"Please tell me you left it at his place after a wicked one-night stand."

Lina laughed. "Not exactly."

Lina filled in most of the details, leaving out the chocolate-mint martini puking incident. As far as she was concerned, it had never happened, and the secret would go with her to her grave. Cassie would never tattle either, and the other bridesmaid in the car had been too drunk to remember the next morning. She doubted Dash would betray such a trust.

"So, what are you going to do tomorrow night?"

She'd been debating it all day. "I don't know."

Tiên pulled her close and flicked Lina's forehead.

"Do not let this guy get away. Climb him like a Christmas tree and live off the memories until you can do it again. This Dash dude might be your perfect match. He even guessed your favorite frappe. Lina, babe, I love you, but don't be a chowderhead."

"Tiên—"

"I am so not kidding. Fuck this man into the new year and deal with the consequences later. You deserve this, and if you're lucky and patient, it might work out."

"How? I spend eleven months out of the year in the far corners of the world, helping people who desperately need it. And I never know where I'm going next."

Tiên took her hands. "You are beautiful, smart, and kind. You will figure it out if it's important to you. And if you're important to him, he'll help you."

There it was. What she was truly afraid of. Was she important enough to this beautiful man for him to tolerate her job, her unavailability? She hadn't found a man with the balls to do so yet. But Tiên was right. There was only one way to figure out if he was boyfriend material, and that was to try.

"Okay, okay. I'll try."

"That's my girl." Tiên hugged her sideways and downed the rest of her drink. "When do your parents get into town?"

"A few days before Christmas. Just enough time to do the shopping and manage the finishing touches. Mom's been doing a lot via email, and Dad's been sending memes."

Tiên rolled her eyes, but in a loving way. She loved Lina's parents almost as much as Lina did, and Tiên had become like a third daughter. She'd been at the bridal shower when Lina could only Zoom in for a few minutes due to the crappy internet. And she would be at the wedding on New Year's Eve. The only reason she hadn't been at the bachelorette party was the aforementioned new baby.

"We'll do lunch the week before the wedding." She glanced at her watch. "Sorry about the movie, babe. I gotta go. Three more days before break, and I have a stack of papers knee-high to grade."

They split the bill, and in a few minutes, Tiên disappeared into the cold New England night. Lina made her way to the condo. Cassie and Wes were curled up on the sofa watching a show with a pretty blond woman in the lead. Her sister stood and joined Lina in the kitchen.

"How's Tiên?"

"Same as always."

"Those poor high school kids. Does the district even know what havoc they've unleashed?"

Cassie poured a glass of wine for herself and held an empty one out for Lina, who shook her head no. She was done drinking for the night.

"She's been there for ten years. The principal must enjoy unleashing chaos gremlins into the greater Boston area."

Their laughter drew Wesley's attention, but he merely smiled as Cassie wiggled her fingers at him and returned to the show.

"Hey, Cass, um, don't expect me home tomorrow night."

A Cheshire cat grin spread over her sister's face, but she wisely said nothing other than, "Thanks for the heads-up."

Lina drank a glass of water and went to bed.

In the morning, she packed her backpack with a toothbrush, deodorant, a change of underwear, and pajamas to sleep in, just in case. Then she spent the day worrying. With a wedding planner in charge, there wasn't much for her to do. The dress would be ready a few days before the wedding, she had found matching shoes, her hair was freshly trimmed, and her parents weren't due in for a few more days. So she was left alone with her thoughts.

And Lina had lots of thoughts. What if she slept with Dash? What if she didn't? What if the whole long-distance thing crashed and burned? And perhaps most vexing, what if it didn't?

She deserved happiness. Everyone deserved happiness. Well, maybe not the shitheads ruining the environment, the warlords killing people, and the politicians willing to screw over their constituents for a tiny piece of the pie. But ordinary, average people deserved happiness.

And Dash could be hers. Something deep in her gut told her he was perfect for her. But years of experience made her leery. She wasn't an overly optimistic twenty-year-old anymore. Lina hadn't given up, but she was more realistic. Developing a relationship where they were only together for a few days or a few weeks at a time was difficult.

Expecting someone to send her into danger might be a bridge too far. Her job could be risky. Those shithead warlords rarely cared who they killed. Generally, they stayed away from aid workers. Kill too many of them and you invite the wrath of the world's biggest military. But sometimes the underlings didn't get the memo.

There was nothing to do but try. She'd promised Tiên, she'd told Cassie, now she needed to promise herself.

Lina spent the rest of the day reading a book and watching her favorite Christmas movies. She cooked a chicken casserole for Wesley, Cassidy, and herself, and said goodbye as soon as her alarm went off at seven-thirty.

Dash sat on the steps leading to the porch, the light over the door illuminating him like a flame-tipped candle. His auburn hair glinted red in the dimness. Dash's ability to go without a hat, scarf, and gloves was a mystery. Even lifelong New Englanders wore those this time of year. Lina wouldn't complain. He was too gorgeous to cover up.

His gaze found her in the shadows, and he hurried down the stairs. Icy fire burned in his eyes as his palm cupped her cheek.

"You came."

"I did. I even brought an overnight bag."

A grin full of promise, full of naughty things, flared on his face as he slid the bag off her shoulder. He took her hand and tugged her toward the back of the house, where another door with a yellow light above it was nestled a few steps into the earth.

Of course, he lived in his parents' basement. Separate entrance. No judgment. He must have a good reason for living with his folks. He was obviously wealthy. This house was not some simple suburban split-level. This was a brownstone, at least 150 years old. If his family owned all of it, they were wealthier than anyone she'd met outside of the fundraising dinners her organization put on.

Dash spun her around so her back was to the door and closed the distance between them. Their breaths made clouds of icy mist, but he still gleamed with yearning and all those delightful, naughty things.

He brought his mouth down upon hers. Soft and sweet for an instant, then demanding. Lina opened for him, and their tongues tangled. A low rumble from him sent tendrils of desire straight between her legs. She reveled in it, reveled in him. He tasted like he would make her every dream come true, with a hint of wintergreen.

Lina closed her eyes, and the world slipped away.

Chapter 13
A Plateful of Sugar Cookies

The streetlamps lit Lina like an angel. A cute, bundled-up, and curvy-as-fuck angel.

She drew Dash like a magnet, like the Pied Piper, like the scent of Christmas cookies. Lina had brought a bag. Triumph coursed through him. She wanted him as much as he wanted her.

He led her to the back door and turned her around, so she wouldn't notice when the magic kicked in. Dash knew he should tell her—he wasn't a fool—but she might think he was delusional. It would be much better to show her. Then she might believe him.

He kissed her. He'd meant it to be a gentle kiss, soft, loving, but the sweet taste of her quickly drove him out of his mind. Dash claimed her with his teeth and his tongue, licking and sucking at her, attempting to devour the quiet noises emerging from her. He was so enraptured, he almost missed his opportunity to open the portal.

But once her eyes closed, he slipped the snowflake key from his pocket and unlocked the door. He guided her inside, the warmth of his room enveloping them. By the time her eyes opened, the magic had vanished. As much as Dash wished to confess, he figured starting with a glowing magic portal to the North Pole might not be a great idea. Showing her around later was the best scheme he could devise, especially with the helpmate bond screaming Lina was his.

He would tell her, but now…well, now seemed the wrong moment to risk it. There was always later.

Dash dropped her bag to the side of the door. The lights were low in his room and a fire flickered in the hearth. He took her hand and led her to the small sofa in front of the fireplace, undoing the buttons on his coat and dropping it to the floor. He sat and unzipped her jacket. She peeled it off and tossed it on top of his, followed by her gloves, scarf, and hat. Dash pulled her onto his lap.

"So, Lina, what do you want for Christmas?"

He tucked a stray strand of hair behind her ear, allowing his fingers to graze her cheek. Her beautiful smile brightened the room, and he hoped he could make her smile like that every day.

"Would it be too corny to say you?" Her thumb traced the edge of his beard, and shivers of desire trembled down his spine.

"No, no, it wouldn't." He turned his head to kiss the finger driving him wild. "You don't have to do anything you don't want to. Just because you're here doesn't mean I expect anything from you, other than your company. And I'm happy to escort you home whenever you wish."

Her palms framed his face, and she kissed him, tentative at first. Dash let her set the pace, keeping his grasp on her rounded hips light and his inner wild man under control. Lina's kiss became demanding, and she pressed her soft breasts into his hard chest, eliciting a low groan from him.

"Silly man," she said breathlessly. "If I didn't want to be here, I wouldn't have come. And if I didn't want to spend the night, I wouldn't have brought the bag. And if I didn't want to fuck you,

I wouldn't have brought a box full of condoms."

Lina yanked her fuzzy sweater off and tossed it behind him, exposing the red lace bra covering her glorious breasts. His hands rose, unbidden, to cup their fullness. Her head dropped back as his thumbs teased her nipples through the lace. He pulled her closer and ran his tongue along the edge of the bra. Tiny whimpers escaped her, driving him into a frenzy of need. His erection pressed hard against his jeans, begging to be released, begging for her.

His fingertips found the bra clasp and freed her breasts. He dragged the straps down her arms, delighting in her silky skin. As soon as he dropped the bra to the ground, his mouth found one sweet nipple. Her fingers threaded through his hair, holding him close.

He sucked and pulled, nibbled and licked. Those tiny whimpers escalated into full-out moans and her hips surged against him, rubbing his cock.

Behind her head, faint blue and silver sparks curled through the air. If he wasn't careful, his own magic would give him away.

"You're killing me, Lina," he murmured hoarsely, leaning back.

An impish grin appeared on her lips. She fumbled with the top button of his shirt and undid it. As her fingers crawled down the row, her eyes shone brighter than the Christmas tree in the Boston Common.

"Am I?"

Her fingernail trailed along his now-exposed chest and goosebumps erupted on his skin. She hooked her finger under the waistband of his jeans and teased the sensitive flesh there.

"Yes." The simple word was part sigh, part hiss, and all lust. Could he let this happen without revealing the truth about himself? He stopped her teasing touch. "I have to tell you something."

Her brow furrowed. "Are you married?"

"God, no!"

"STI?"

"No."

She held a finger over his lips. "Then it can wait."

Dash growled low in frustration, but he wanted her. Postponing the discussion wasn't the best course of action, but he would tell her before she went home.

Lina distracted him, teased him, and he thrust up as her fingers grazed his hard cock through the layers of clothes. She licked her lips, and for an instant, the ability to reason left him. All he could imagine were those delectable lips wrapped around his hard length. Another time. Please, let there be another time.

Lina leaned in, pressing her breasts to his naked chest. His arm snaked around her back and held her in place. She trailed kisses from his neck to his ear, nibbling on the lobe.

"Do you know how wet I am? Just for you," she whispered.

He turned his head and captured her mouth, his tongue dipping in and out, tasting her, as his hands edged down her spine and slid under her leggings. He caressed her round, beautiful ass, holding her still as he arched into her.

"Damn these clothes," he said with a growl.

"There's a simple solution."

Her fingers dropped to his jeans again and flicked open the button. She found the zipper and pulled it down, stroking his cock through his boxer briefs.

That was enough. Dash surged forward and pressed her into the sofa. He stood, dropped his shirt, and pulled off his jeans and underwear in a few quick movements. Kneeling beside the sofa, he pulled a wrapped condom from his jean pocket. He held it out to Lina.

"Whenever you're ready."

She took the condom from him with another naughty smile.

"What if I'm ready now?"

"I think you'll want to hold off a bit."

He grabbed the waistband of her leggings and pulled them off. She wore a matching red thong, the lace hiding nothing. Fuck, she was more tempting than a plateful of sugar cookies.

Dash slid a finger under the edge near her hip and ran it along until he brushed over her mound. He brought his face next to her thigh and blew a cold breath over her sex. Her voluptuous hips bucked, and a chuckle slipped out of him.

"You like that?"

"Yesss," she hissed, twisting her hands into his hair. "More."

His finger found her clit and flicked it. Her hips rose once more. Before she lowered them, he snagged her thong and yanked it off. He buried his face between her thighs.

Finding her clit with his tongue, he gave it the same attention as he had her breasts. Sucking, licking, nibbling until she pulled his hair tight. It hurt so good. She was so wet for him and tasted better than anything he'd eaten before. He could spend his life between her thighs and die a happy man.

"Now, Dash," she said, tugging him away.

He wiped his face with his hand and licked his lips, relishing her taste. Lina fumbled with the wrapper but managed to open it and pull out the condom. She unrolled it along his hard length. Catching her bottom lip with her teeth, she looked positively naughty as she peered at him. The fire lit her brown hair with red highlights, the curls framing her in a dark halo, and her eyes—dear lord, her eyes were aflame with lust and longing.

As soon as her hands left his cock, he gently shoved her into her corner of the sofa, bracing on the arm on either side of her head. She guided him home. He slid into her, as smooth as silk, and her hips rose to meet him, inviting him in as deep as he could go. Her low moan mingled with his satisfied growl.

"Everything good?" he asked.

"Kiss me," she demanded, snaking her hand behind his head and pulling him down.

"Your wish is my command," he mumbled against her lips before closing the gap.

He bruised her mouth with his desire, pushed his tongue inside as he rolled his hips against her. She brushed her tongue against his and met his thrust. Dash dragged a hand along her body, stopping to massage her pillowy breast before burning a trail down to where their bodies joined.

He found her clit again and flicked it, swallowing her gasp at the sensation. Rubbing it in a circular motion in time with his rolling hips, Dash had her panting on the edge of climax.

"Come for me, Lina."

He pinched her clit and claimed her mouth again as she broke. She clenched around him and her hips lifted off the couch, seating him deep inside her. It was what he needed. He spilled over his own edge, wildly thrusting into her as pleasure exploded all around him in a miniature aurora borealis, greens and blues and pinks spiraling through the air. Thankfully, her eyes were closed as she came down from her own orgasm.

A nebulous cloak of wellbeing surrounded his heart and his mind, a sensation he'd never before experienced after sex. For a moment, all was right with the world. The helpmate bond had been sealed. Oh, boy. How in the hell was he going to explain that?

The little light show dissipated before Lina noticed, leaving only a shimmer to the air. He kissed her gently and she stroked his hair.

"That was…" She giggled and shook her head. "I don't have words."

"Good, that means I did my job."

Her giggle turned into a laugh. He slid out of her, and he pushed away from the sofa. He grabbed the fuzzy blanket on the sofa and covered her.

"Stay right there. I'm going to clean up."

"I couldn't move if I wanted to."

Dash hurried to the bathroom, took care of his needs, and brought back a warm washcloth for her. He knelt in front of her once again and cleaned her. Then he scooped her in his arms, blanket and all, and carried her to his bed. Where she belonged, where they belonged.

He crawled in and pulled Lina against him. She was the little spoon to his big spoon, and he'd never felt he was right where he was supposed to be until this moment. Lina was his helpmate, and come sleet, snow, or the end of the fucking world, he would love and protect her.

She threaded her fingers through his and brought them to her lips for a soft kiss. Clasping his hand to her chest, Lina snuggled closer. Dash stroked her hair until they both fell asleep.

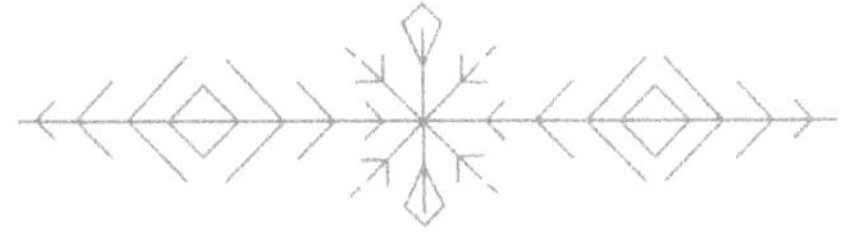

CHAPTER 14
TOURIST IN THE KITCHEN

The clock on the bedside table read a few minutes past three when Lina woke again, thirsty. Dash's breath tickled the hair on her neck, and she shivered in delight.

"Mmm." He kissed the spot just below her ear. "I like when you do that."

His erection poked her in the back.

"I can tell. I'd be more than happy to oblige, but I'm thirsty."

"Okay, hold that thought."

He swung his long, lanky legs out of bed and walked naked to a small fridge tucked under a wet bar on the far side of the room. Lina hadn't noticed it when they first arrived, too focused on him, on them, on the fiery desire flooding her system.

Afterward, something had clicked in her mind as she had nestled in with him last night. A deep peace settled around her, a connection she'd never experienced with another person before. Leaving him would be hard, and a tinge of sadness muted her happiness at being here.

Dash pulled out two bottles of water. "Are you hungry?"

"A little." Lina pushed away the melancholy. She was here with him now, and it was worth celebrating.

He grabbed a small plate and rummaged in the cupboard. She enjoyed the view of his tight ass. As he returned, his cock was still at half-mast, but when his gaze locked on her, it twitched in anticipation. Lina couldn't help the slow, sultry smile at the evidence of how much he desired her.

"You keep flirting with me, and I won't give you a chance to eat your snack," he said as he slid under the covers.

She snagged a water bottle from him, twisted off the cap, and gulped a good third of the contents. He watched her with eyebrows raised.

"What? I haven't had a workout like that in way too long, mister."

Dash set the plate between them, a selection of sliced cheese and some crackers. He cracked open his own water and sipped. "That's a damn shame."

She picked up a slice of yellow cheese and a cracker and popped it in her mouth. Eating cheese and crackers in Hottie McBartender's bed was the ultimate indulgence. Lina washed down the snack with another gulp of water.

He had another cracker prepped for her, holding it out with a sweet smile. She let him feed it to her.

"Gotta keep up your strength." He eyed her in a way that made her feel beautiful and cherished.

Mouth suddenly dry, she sipped her water. Lina didn't want cheese and crackers anymore. There was only one thing she wanted between her lips, and it had nothing to do with dairy or carbs.

Dash held out another cracker, but she shook her head. Lina took a last sip of water, recapped her bottle, and placed it on the nightstand.

"That's not what I want to eat right now."

She slid her hand over his chest and firmly grasped his cock. He hissed in a breath and stilled as she pumped him once, twice.

Lina took the plate and set it beside her water. Dash capped his own bottle and let it drop over the side of the bed.

Capturing her lips with his own, he groaned as she worked her hand up and down his hard length. She broke away and burrowed under the covers. Lina crawled between his legs and lowered her mouth over the tip of his cock.

"Fuck, Lina…"

She hummed around his girth, and his words trailed off into a rumble that sent heat straight to her core. Pumping him with one hand, she sucked him down while bracing herself with her other. Her thighs grew slick. Dash thrust himself into her mouth, and she smiled around him. The power she had over him was a huge turn-on.

"Please," he groaned. "I can't take much more."

She pulled back the covers, and met his crystalline eyes, alight with desire for her. Lina could lose herself in their wintry depths and never once care what she traded for the privilege. Dash fumbled in the drawer of his nightstand until he pulled out another condom. She worked it slowly, ever so slowly, over his cock. He groaned and thrust, impatient and frustrated.

"Tell me what you want, Dash." She hovered over his cock, surprised at the joy such power brought her. She didn't need his answer, though—the same connectedness from last night answered it for her, but she waited for it anyway.

"To come inside you."

She grasped his base and lowered herself over him, inch by delicious inch. He filled her just right, and she sighed as the fullness registered.

Dash cupped her breasts, rubbing his thumbs over her nipples. Lina rose and fell over him, letting his shaft rub against her clit. The heat grew low in her belly and she tilted her head back, riding him. Dash made her feel safe and valued and in control.

The balloon burst and she relinquished her control, pleasure shattering her.

"Lina, oh god," he said as he exploded inside her.

Swirling spirals of color surrounded them, bringing with it the scent of snow and evergreen. She'd never come so hard she hallucinated. Lina collapsed onto his chest.

Dash stroked her hair as their heart rates returned to normal.

"Mmm, Dash?"

"Yes?"

"That was amazing." She wasn't about to inform him it was the most amazing sex she ever had. No need to give Hottie McBartender an even larger ego.

He tipped her head with a finger under her chin and smiled sleepily. "Yes, it was."

"I wish…"

Lina tried to grasp the ephemeral concepts flying around her head. She wished they could be like this forever. She wished he could come with her when she returned to Greece. She wished she didn't have to leave. But they couldn't stay here forever, he couldn't come with her, and she would have to leave. A hush fell over the room.

"I know." Dash pressed his lips to hers, softly. He rolled her over and tucked her into the covers. "Be right back."

He was, once again with a warm washcloth. Since they'd used a condom, it wasn't a big, sticky mess, but the warmth felt nice against her all too often unused lady bits. He crawled in and pulled her against him.

"Sleep well, Lina," he rumbled, his palm resting over her breast.

Too satiated to be turned on by it, she found it comforting. Soon, his breathing slowed, but Lina couldn't sleep.

She slipped out of his embrace and dressed. Grabbing what was left of her water, she padded to the sofa and sat in front of the dying embers of the fire. She finished the water, and her belly grumbled. She'd been too nervous to eat much, and only had a couple of crackers with cheese. After spending almost the entire night here, Lina finally examined her surroundings.

There was the old-fashioned fireplace, with its cast iron firebox and wooden mantel. A stack of perfectly cut hardwood sat to one side, ready to be used. The walls were an off-white plaster and nice paintings, possibly prints, were framed and hung with care. Classic artists, nothing past the Impressionists.

The hardwood floors were warm against her unstockinged feet as she moved quietly about the large room. A sofa and two plush armchairs sat in front of the fireplace, a small wet bar was on the far wall with the dorm fridge and microwave, and the huge king-size bed took up another wall. The bathroom, where Dash had disappeared twice to clean up, opened onto the bedroom, with a door for the toilet tucked into the far corner.

Wait, there was only one other door, the door they'd come through. How did he get into the main house? Outside and back in through a different door? Inefficient, but all Dash had mentioned was he had his own entrance. The light leaking in from under the outside door appeared off, too. It had been golden and incandescent when she had arrived at the brownstone, but was now cooler, more LED-ish.

Curiosity got the best of her, and she opened the door. She expected the cold Boston night, but a richly painted, wainscoted hallway greeted her.

The hell?

Then it dawned on her. She was dreaming. Her brain was processing the details of the room and making up other shit. Strange, she'd never experienced lucid dreaming before.

The floor was surprisingly warm against her feet as she made her way along the hall, which curved oddly. The top half of the walls were painted a rich blue, and the wainscoting was a lustrous white, almost like snow under a clear winter sky.

Lina followed the curve of the wall past closed doors until a large, dimly lit opening appeared, leading into a well-appointed modern kitchen. Huge stainless-steel appliances, a small but sturdy kitchen table, and a butcher block island surrounded by simple, white barstools greeted her. She stepped into the room, running her hand along the white marble countertops. Someone had left on the light over the range.

"Who the fuck are you?"

The voice came from the doorway where a young woman about her age, a little taller with blond curls, stood. Her eyes gleamed furiously in the dim light. There was something familiar about her. For finding a stranger in her kitchen, the woman wasn't frightened at all.

She peered at Lina for a moment before horror spread over her face.

"You're human! Some chucklehead decided to show off to their latest conquest. I'm going to have their balls on a platter."

She pulled a phone from her pocket and dialed.

"Sorry, do I know you?" Lina asked. This was a strange turn for the dream to take.

"No, you don't know me. That's the fucking problem, lady." Someone on the other end of the phone must've answered. "We've got a tourist in the kitchen. Get here as fast as you can."

The woman tucked her phone back in her pocket and looked Lina up and down, shaking her head.

"Not your fault." She approached the island and pulled out a barstool. "Have a seat and we'll sort this all out."

Lina leaned into the weird narrative of this dream. Why not sit and talk with the rude, sweary woman who'd called…*someone* on her? Cops? No, it sounded more like a security guard. She settled onto the stool.

Feet pounded down the hallway, and two things happened at

once. A Black man dressed in a uniform resembling the British military of the eighteenth century burst through the open doors, panting. Though gray sprinkled his hair, he moved with a nearly hypnotic grace. And his ears…they were pointed, as if he was something out of an epic fantasy.

What the hell had her chicken casserole done to her imagination? Or was it her recent binge-watch of *The Lord of the Rings*?

At the same time the strange man arrived, so did Dash, though it took a moment for Lina to register his presence. The new man took all her attention as she tried to figure out what was happening. As the guard approached, a shirtless Dash threw himself between them. The man stopped short and confusion crossed his face as he glanced between the woman and Dash.

"She's with me." Dash's words echoed too loudly in the kitchen.

Lina blinked. Wait, this was real? She pinched her forearm hard.

"Ow." Yes, this was real, but there was no way she was in an old Boston brownstone. Wesley's parents lived in one, and there were no weird, curving hallways in their house. And where the fuck were the windows? The city noises?

Dash glanced at her. "You okay, Lina?"

"Dash, where am I? And how the hell did we get here?"

"You didn't tell her?" The woman's voice grew cold and her nostrils flared.

"Joy, Dash, what am I supposed to be doing?" asked the guard.

Dash rested a hand on his arm. "Thank you, Hugo, but this is a private matter. Lina Schultz is my guest. I'll handle her."

"Handle me?" Lina's fists found her hips, and her chest heaved with the effort of corralling her anger.

Dash flinched. "Please, Lina, give me a minute—"

One, two, three… She was confused, frightened, and together those things made her livid. Dash had, what, kidnapped her, lied to her. Whatever the truth was, he respected her too little to speak it. And what the fuck was a creature from Middle Earth doing in his kitchen? Elves weren't even real. She could storm out, but where would she go? The doors in his room led here or the bathroom. Deep breath and *four, five, six…*

Lina unclenched her fists and crossed her arms, giving him her best imitation of her Granny's death stare that had one message: *you messed up*.

Dash swallowed before addressing the guard, Hugo. "I'll explain things and make sure Lina gets home safely."

Hugo looked at Joy, raising his eyebrows. She pointed a thumb at Dash.

"It's my brother's mess. I guess we should let him clean it up."

"I. Am not. Someone's. *Mess*," Lina spit out.

Dash reached for her, but she pulled away. No way was the asshole going to touch her right now. He didn't deserve it.

"I apologize, Lina." Joy's eyes gleamed with sympathy. Lina now understood why the woman had looked familiar. She had the same color eyes as her brother, and Joy's face, though softer and more feminine, reminded Lina of Dash. "I meant the situation is a mess, not you. My brother fucked up, and I'm sorry you were caught in the middle of it. Come on, Hugo."

Hugo followed Joy out of the kitchen. Dash stepped in her direction.

"Don't," Lina barked.

His shoulders slumped, but he respected her boundary. "Can I make you some cocoa?"

"No, Dash. All I want is to know where the fuck I am and how you managed to bring me here. And then I want to go home."

He nodded and sat on the barstool on the opposite end of the island, giving her the distance she needed and removing the temptation to reach out to her again.

Dash heaved a huge sigh and folded his hands in front of him. He looked straight at her, sadness gleaming in the icy blue depths of his eyes.

"I'm sorry, Lina. My intention was to tell you as soon as we got here. I know intentions are worth shit, and I allowed myself to get…distracted. I was not going to keep this from you any longer."

When he paused, the silence hanging heavy over them, she prodded. "Keep what from me?"

He leaned his head against his folded hands. "I thought you might not believe me if you didn't see it for yourself."

"You're still not making any sense, Dash." The peace from before she slept was long gone, leaving only a confusing mess of frustration, anger, and disappointment. "One more chance to tell me where I am, or I'll find Hugo and ask him to explain what a fictional species is doing in your parents' kitchen."

"You're at the North Pole."

"Fuck you!" She jumped up from the stool.

"I swear. Do you have your phone on you?"

She stopped. "No, it's in your room."

"Give me a minute. Sit, please."

Lina leaned against the island, arms crossed over her chest, and scowled at him. He rubbed the bridge of his nose, walked over to the switches on the wall, and hit the middle one. A whirring noise above her head pulled her attention to the ceiling. There was a frosted skylight in the middle of the room, but the glass was separating, leaving a clear view into the night sky through another pane of unfrosted glass.

Ribbons of green, blue, and lavender undulated through the midnight sky, the twinkling distant stars peeking through the light show. Aurora borealis. Not usually visible in Boston, as far as she knew, only the most northern latitudes like…the North Pole.

"If you had your phone, the GPS would show you on the northern-most point of Greenland."

"I thought you said it was the North Pole."

"You can't build a setup like this on the ice cap. But the name stuck."

"Why…what…how?" The lights were magnificent, but the physical impossibility of traveling this far in a single step through a door took her words away.

"Welcome to Santa's workshop. He's my dad."

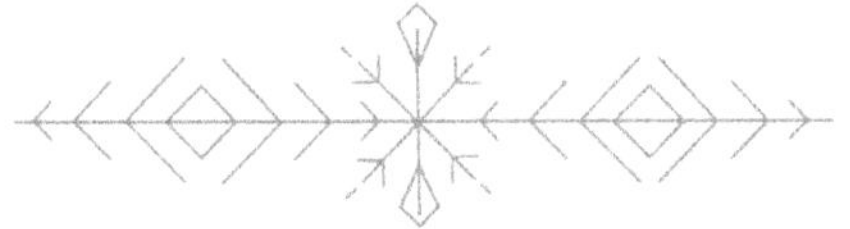

CHAPTER 15
SANTA NUMBER ELEVEN

Yeah, maybe that wasn't the best way to break the news to Lina. But how would anybody tell the woman they just banged they were thousands of miles from home and, by the way, Santa Claus is real?

Lina peered at him as though searching for the lie. Her shoulders were hunched forward and tight, her whole body was stiff. But when she found only the truth in his face, a tiny fraction of the tension bled away.

"You expect me to believe that?"

Dash ran his hands through his hair. "There's my problem. If I had told you last night before bringing you here, would you have believed me?"

He had allowed himself to become distracted, his previous experience with a human coloring his judgment. Now he was facing the consequences of his actions.

"You didn't give me a chance."

"Would you have believed me?"

Lina wouldn't meet his gaze.

"So, no," he said, deflated.

Not that he blamed her. The elves had worked hard at

making everybody believe they were a myth. But a part of him hoped their helpmate bond might override the natural skepticism of her human nature. Which was another thing he needed to explain. One deep, dark secret at a time.

"But your ears—"

"Are glamoured. A simple magic spell to make them look human. Would you care to touch them, see for yourself?"

She shook her head. Dash muttered the Old Norse word to remove the spell. A little flash of golden sparkles, and his ears were back to normal. Lina gasped and covered her mouth with a hand.

"I'm an elf. My parents are elves. And before you comment about my height, we're talking old-school Germanic elves from folklore, not cute cartoons selling cookies."

He ran the odds of what her next question would be. Santa or the reindeer?

"How?" she asked, surprising him. "How did you bring me here?"

"Magic. There's a key. Turn it in any door, and it will take you where you want to go. Last night, I wanted you in my bed, so here we are."

Dash made a broad gesture, encompassing the compound. Lina had only seen the family residence in her nighttime foray. There were the offices on the other half of the topside dome, not to mention the several levels below ground and the stables.

"And your father is Santa?" Her words were slow and careful, as though she couldn't believe she uttered them.

"Yes. My dad's name is Ivan. Santa Claus is more a title than a name." He bit his lip, trying to do the math. "He's the ninth…no, the tenth Santa Claus. Elves live about twice as long as humans."

"So someday you'll be Santa number eleven?"

"That's their plan."

"But not yours."

Dash shrugged. It didn't matter what his plan was. His future had been laid out for him, all nice and neat and candy cane sweet.

"This is…a lot," she said after a moment of quiet.

"I know, and I'm sorry. I should have told you before bringing you here. You deserved to make the choice, and I took it away from you."

"You did, and I'm angry about it."

Lina's voice carried no anger, though.

"Is there a but to that sentence?" he asked quietly.

She finally looked at him. "Not exactly. I need to process this, Dash, work through my anger. Part of me wants to believe you when you say you planned on telling me—the part that vaguely remembers you said you had something to tell me. I was a bit distracted. Part of me wonders if you're apologizing only because you got caught. And the rest of me is trying to wrap my head around the fact that not only is Santa real, but I just fucked his son."

Lina snorted. The snort turned into a chuckle, then a laugh. An edge of madness crept in, and tears streamed down her cheeks. Still, Dash respected the boundary she set at the beginning of their conversation. As much as he would like to take her in his arms and comfort her, that wasn't what she needed right now.

Instead, he found his mother's stash of tissues in a drawer and passed the box to her. She took a few deep breaths and dabbed away the tears.

"My parents arrive tomorrow." She twisted the tissue. "Will you meet me at The Old Bell the day after at two?"

"Anytime and anywhere, Lina."

She pushed off from the island and uncrossed her arms. "I want to go home now."

"Of course. Your things and my key are in my room. Are you okay going back there with me, or would you prefer I bring everything here?"

She turned the possibilities over in her mind but decided quickly. "I don't want to be here longer than I have to."

Dash's heart fell. God, that hurt, but he only had himself to blame. He should have told her last night. He led the way to his room. Lina gathered her things quickly, oh so quickly. He had gone to sleep filled with hope for his future, but now his future was balled up in the trash like a bad financial report, lucky it wasn't on fire. He deserved for it to burn, yet Lina had enough grace to grant him some time.

"I'm ready," she said after a last look around his room.

Dash snagged the key from the little table by the door. "I haven't been to your sister's place yet, so I'm going to need to touch you for the magic to work. Picture where you want to go."

He held out his hand. Lina rested her hand on his, as if she touched the prickly needles of a noble fir, and Dash did not close his fingers. The worst thing he could do right now was force more contact than she was comfortable with.

The doorway glowed and a keyhole appeared. Dash inserted the key and opened the door.

A long, modern hallway greeted them. Lina snatched her hand away, but awe painted her face. She walked through the door and stopped at an apartment about halfway down the hall. As he was about to close the door, she glanced over her shoulder at him and nodded.

Then she entered the condo, and he was alone. But maybe, her nod meant something. Just maybe, she could forgive him.

He shut the door and the glow faded. That could have gone better. Of course, it could have gone much, much worse. Only time would tell if he blew his shot at true happiness.

CHAPTER 16
GEE THANKS, DAD

She tossed and turned, the events of the night crowding her mind. With a single step, she'd traversed thousands of miles. Those sparkling lights she assumed had been a hallucination—were they real? Was any of this real?

The only thing Lina was sure of at the moment was Dash had kept secrets, hadn't valued her enough to trust her. Once again, she hadn't been enough. This time, it didn't just hurt her feelings. It hurt her soul.

When the sun rose around seven, she heard Cassie banging pans in the kitchen. Finally, she fell asleep. The next time she woke, it was three in the afternoon and the condo was silent. Both Cassie and Wes were off to work. She dragged her ass out of bed for some water and ibuprofen.

The shower washed away her physical aches, but being alone with her thoughts did nothing for her emotional pain. She replayed the events of the last week, wondering if she could have guessed. In retrospect, a few clues were there, but Dash was skillful in how he answered questions, and to be honest, she hadn't been looking for double entendres. At least, not that kind.

When she emerged from the shower, dressed but looking like

three-day-old leftovers, Cassie was in the kitchen, cooking dinner. She looked up with a sly grin as Lina slunk down the hall.

"How was last night?" Cassie's grin faded as Lina entered the brightly lit kitchen. "You look like shit."

Lina poured herself another glass of water and drank half of it straight away. "Thanks for the compliment. And I don't want to talk about it."

Cassie pressed her lips together, and for a second Lina expected she was going to insist on talking about it. But her sister kept her mouth shut and busied herself with chopping vegetables.

Lina grabbed a piece of fruit from the bowl in the middle of the island and ate it. Her stomach roiled, but she forced it down and felt a little better for it. Cassie soon joined her.

"When does Wes get home?" Lina sipped her remaining water.

Her sister glanced at the clock on the stove. "Soon, though he might be a little late." A wicked smile played with the corners of her sister's mouth. "He overslept this morning. Since we had the condo to ourselves last night, we—"

Lina covered her ears and hummed loudly, but she was glad at least someone got what they deserved last night. She finished her water, feeling better at last. Whatever Cassie had cooking smelled divine.

"When are we picking up Mom and Dad tomorrow?"

Cassie glanced at the clock on the stove. "Their flight arrives around three. Assuming it's on time, we should leave here no later than 2:30."

"Great." Nearly twenty-four hours to mope.

"You sure you don't want to talk about what happened with Dash last night?"

Where would she even begin? *I'm dating Santa's son and he*

kidnapped me to the North Pole would surely earn her an involuntary psychiatric hold. Which may have been Dash's point of not divulging his secret to her, but she was still pissed. Lina needed a bit of time to think about how to phrase her issue without sounding delusional. She wanted to come clean to Cassie. Her sister was surprisingly insightful for an ungrateful, bratty younger sibling.

"I'll make you a deal—you don't bring it up again, and I'll tell you in the car after supper tomorrow."

Cassie licked her hand and stuck it out. "Spit promise."

Lina did the same and they shook on it.

She fell asleep by midnight but spent the next day trying and failing to read her book. Too much churned in her brain to allow her to get lost in a story. Cassie came to collect her about a quarter after two.

They waited by the baggage claim. Lina bounced on her toes, looking for her dad's lanky form and her mother's cardinal red coat. A hat with an obnoxious orange pom caught her attention, sitting atop the very man she'd been scanning the crowd for. Her mother trailed behind, the color of her signature coat flashing through breaks in the crowd.

And in seconds, her dad's loving arms pulled her in for a tight hug while her mother squeezed the life out of Cassie. They switched, and her mom's soft powdery fragrance filled Lina's senses. There was nothing like a mother's embrace.

"Pete, let me grab the bags. You heard the physical therapist." Her mother gave him a playful shove toward his daughters and disappeared into the crowd awaiting their baggage.

"What physical therapist?" Lina asked.

"Old shoulder injury. Trying therapy first to avoid surgery. Therapist suggested keeping the lifting to a minimum for a few weeks and work on exercises."

"Must suck for your golf game," Cassie said.

"A little." He draped an arm around her shoulders. "But the guys said I could drive the cart and keep score until I could play again."

"They may end up regretting both of those." Lina smirked affectionately. Her dad was a notoriously aggressive driver and couldn't add without a calculator to save his life.

"Shh, don't tell anyone."

They were still laughing when her mother returned with the two bags. Lina took one, Cassie the other.

"What are you all laughing about?" Her mom glanced between them.

"Dad's golfing buddies."

"Oh, he told you his new duties." Her familiar smile filled Lina with peace.

They chatted as they moved through the crowd until they got to Cassie's car.

"Enjoying your vacation?" her mom asked as she and Lina sat in the back seat.

"Mostly. I puked on a guy's boots."

Lynn winced. "Ooh, rough. What else?"

"He asked me out on a date anyway."

"Like him already. Not afraid of risk. Did you say yes?"

Lina giggled in spite of herself. The spark of hope on her mom's face kept Lina from revealing the current situation.

"Yeah, I did."

"And?"

"And it's only been a week, and I'm not discussing my dating life with my mom the first time I've seen her in months."

"Fair enough, but tomorrow…"

"Fine. I'll fill you in tomorrow at the bridal shop."

After she met with Dash. After she figured out what she was going to do about the whole situation.

The Schultzes were staying with Wesley's parents. They pulled in front of the old Federal-style row house in Beacon Hill. Wesley was already there, waiting for them. He came out to help with the bags and showed Lynn and Peter to their room. Arthur and Elizabeth Blackworth both hugged Cassie.

"It's good to see you again, Lina. How is your work in Greece going?" Elizabeth ushered them inside, out of the cold.

"Things have stabilized for a bit, and we're able to provide more consistent services to the refugees."

Lina hung her coat in the small closet of the foyer, tucking her un-ridiculous hat, scarf, and gloves into a sleeve. She missed her granny hat almost as much as the woman who had made it.

"Well, that's great, isn't it, Ellie?" Arthur said, a little too enthusiastically.

"Yes, so promising. Does that mean you'll be returning stateside soon?"

"Unfortunately, there's always more refugees. Once we've helped this batch, another is right behind. But I'm about due for a turn in admin, and the headquarters of the organization is in DC, so it's possible. That's one of the things I love about this job. I never know where I'll end up next."

"Ooh, you'd be able to pursue something with Hottie McBartender," Cassie said with a smile.

"A bartender? Surely you can do better, a lovely girl like you." Arthur patted her shoulder awkwardly.

The Blackworths weren't bad people, but they hadn't quite been able to shake their elitist streak. Should she inform them he wasn't just a bartender, or should she let them stew?

Elizabeth saved her, taking Lina aback. "Arthur, we've talked about this. Work is work, and we shouldn't judge people by their profession."

"Yes, you're right. My apologies, Lina. If he is, in fact, a—what did Cassie call him—right, a hottie, then go get him."

Cassie rolled her eyes behind him, and Lina could no longer suppress her smile.

"Thanks, Arthur, but a few thousand miles can put a damper on a new relationship."

Elizabeth led the way to an honest-to-god sitting room. All antique furniture, and only some of it comfortable. Wesley and her parents soon joined them, and Arthur served drinks from a cart stationed at the far end of the room. An older woman in an apron appeared about thirty minutes later to announce dinner was served. The lovely scent of herbed chicken and potatoes filled the air, with a crisp green salad and rolls waiting on separate plates.

It was as delightful as it smelled, and Lina ate every bite.

They sat and chatted for a long while after the dishes were cleared until Cassie glanced at her watch.

"We're heading back to the condo. See you tomorrow for the dress fitting, Mom?"

Her mother smiled. "Sure thing. I have the address and will be there promptly at three."

"Lovely." Elizabeth rose to escort them out.

Soon enough, Lina and Cassie were in her car, with Wes a few minutes behind. Dread filled her. She still hadn't figured out how to tell her sister about Dash without revealing who Dash really was. But for the last several years, Cassie had been a reliable sounding board, even more so since she'd graduated law school.

"Time to spill, Lina. You've had me worried for two days."

Lina studied her sister, tapping her leg. "I can't tell you everything, because the story isn't all mine to tell."

"Okay…"

"Dash told me a family secret I wasn't expecting and could have some interesting consequences on any future we might have together."

"Vague much? What could be so bad? A kid with an ex? You like kids. Juvie? He's obviously put that part of his past behind him. Rocky relationship with the parents? We've got enough parental love to share."

"It's not any of those."

If only it was a kid with an ex. As complicated as those kinds of relationships could be for everyone involved, they would still be easier than explaining to her family Santa Claus was real and she wasn't having hallucinations. She wouldn't have to explain anything if she called things off with him, but damn, she missed him after less than forty-eight hours.

She craved the peace he brought her before she found out the truth.

The only sound in the car for a good five minutes was the Christmas music from the easy listening station.

"I don't have advice for you, Lina, not without specifics." She held up a hand before Lina could protest. "And I understand you can't give them to me. But I have a question for you to consider, and an observation."

"Gee, thanks, Dad." The sarcasm dripped from Lina's words.

This was a tried-and-true technique in the Schultz household. If you couldn't give advice, for any reason, you asked a question that might lead the person to a solution. And you offered an observation to help them put things in context.

"You know it works."

"Yeah, that's what makes me so irritated."

Their soft laughter filled the car, drowning out the music for a bit.

"Fine," Lina said. "Go ahead. Pull a Schultz."

"When is a good time to tell the person you're dating a family secret?" Cassie spared her a quick glance.

Certainly before taking her to the fucking North Pole without her permission. But she acknowledged the point with a nod. If his dad had been a billionaire rather than Santa Claus, when would she expect him to admit it? Wait—was Santa a billionaire? This was hard.

"You've known each other, what, a week?"

"Eight days. Is that the observation? Because I can count."

Cassie snorted. "No, you tool. Here's your observation. The dude still asked you on a date, even though you puked chocolate-mint martini all over his boots. Like, that's fiancé behavior, not random-stranger-you-met-in-a-bar behavior. And that's all I got, sis."

She wasn't wrong. Not one bit. Still kissing someone after they'd puked on you wasn't just boyfriend material, it was husband material. A frisson passed through her, though the question remained whether it was fear or anticipation over the possibility of having everything she ever wished for.

"Thanks, Cass."

"Anytime. You're not the first Schultz to need a kick in the pants when it comes to their love life."

Lina leaned her head against the window as they pulled into the parking garage. Dash Nichols made her feel valued and appreciated in a way few had. When she was with him, the rest of the world vanished. And he was hot as hell. The orgasms weren't a bad side benefit, either.

Was she seriously considering dating Hottie McBartender, aka Son of Santa?

Yes, yes, she was.

CHAPTER 17
RUMOR AND RESTAURANTS

Dash's stomach roiled all damn day. He'd opened the bar at nine and had been doing anything and everything to keep his mind off Lina's visit.

What if she rejected him? To the best of his knowledge, no helpmates had ever rejected each other. It was a...compulsion was too strong a word, but longing fit pretty well, with a side of occasional fixation. Whatever her decision, though, she was it for him. If she decided to have nothing to do with him, he would never marry, never have kids. Hell, he might never date again. His right hand would get a workout. At least his one night with her could provide enough fuel for his imagination for the rest of his life.

As two o'clock approached, Dash found a hundred little things that needed doing. Citrus to be sliced, ice hoppers to be filled, tables to clear and wipe down.

"What's gotten into you today, boss?" Julia dried off a pint glass and looked him over with an expression resembling motherly concern. "I haven't seen you this fidgety since the rumor went round about the reviewer coming in."

He collapsed on a barstool. Ugh, that had been a bitch of a

week, always guessing which patron might be reviewing them for a magazine or newspaper. Turned out the answer was none, but rumor and restaurants went hand in hand like holly and ivy.

"I may have fucked up things with Lina."

Julia's demeanor invited confession. She was a good bartender, had a motherly streak, and wasn't his actual mother.

"Lina? Oh, the hat chick. Did you ever find it for her?"

"No, but I asked her out on a couple of dates. The last one didn't go as I hoped. She found out something about me before I could tell her."

Julia hissed a breath in through her teeth. "Ouch. That's never good."

"Tell me about it."

"Well, at least you know you messed up. A lot of guys wouldn't even recognize it, let alone admit it. What are you going to do?"

"She asked for time but agreed to meet me today."

"Ah, waiting for the other shoe. Got it. Need me to hang some mistletoe?"

Dash chuckled sadly. "Doubt it'll help, but if it makes you feel better…"

"I'll put a reserved sign on the table in the far corner—give you two some privacy."

If she sticks around long enough. But he thanked Julia, grateful for her sympathy.

Hat chick. Huh. In his eagerness to woo her, and his despondency since the other night, Dash had forgotten all about the hat that had brought Lina back to the bar. If he could find her hat, perhaps he could make some amends for his poor judgment. Even if she rejected him now, she might appreciate the gesture later. And he could always send it anonymously.

He needed to speak with Joy. His sister had a much better grasp on elven magic than he did. She would know a spell, a ritual, or a magical creature that could find things. Surely, if humans could train dogs to sniff out any number of things, there had to be some sort of magical equivalent.

All thought of the hat with the green pom went out the door when her voice broke through his navel-gazing.

"Hi, Dash."

It was carefully neutral but still set his heart to racing, his palms to sweating, and his cock to twitching. *Down, boy.*

He turned his head and flashed a quick smile. He couldn't help it—he was so glad to see her, so glad she hadn't stood him up, though she had every right to.

"Hi, Lina. Thanks for coming."

"I said I'd be here. But I can't stay long. I'm supposed to meet my mom and Cassie at the bridal shop at three." She pulled off her gloves and unzipped her coat.

"Okay. Do you want to talk here, or would you like more privacy?"

Dash was unsure which would be the worse choice. If she was going to dump his ass, might as well do it here and get it over with. But she might try to spare his feelings by insisting on more privacy. On the other hand, if she wanted to talk more, it could mean she might forgive him. Ugh, he had never been this waffly, this vulnerable, with anybody else. This helpmate bond was a son of a bitch.

Lina glanced around. The Old Bell wasn't busy, but there were a few people at the bar.

"Somewhere more private," she said.

He led her to the table with the reserved tent, a cozy two-top nestled in a corner. After they sat, she took in a deep breath, but just sat there, as though she couldn't force out words.

"Would it help if I apologized again?" he asked. "Because I am sorry, and not because I got caught. I'm sorry I wasn't brave enough to tell you the truth, and my cowardice caused you pain.

I should have told you before whisking you away."

Lina took his hand, and Dash suppressed the shiver threatening to travel throughout his entire body, leaving him in a puddle on the floor. Such a simple touch and it had him ready to kneel at her feet, pledging forever. Had it crossed his mind in the last five minutes how much this bond sucked?

"Dash, it's okay. It seems little sisters aren't just annoying. They sometimes point out the obvious and offer good advice." A smile crept across her lips, and she rolled her eyes theatrically. "Apparently, it's considered socially acceptable to not tell someone you've known for a week your deepest, darkest secrets."

His heart soared. She forgave him, and she was smiling at him—a genuine smile, not an awkward grimace if she were dumping his ass. He returned it, but kept his enthusiasm in check, in case he was reading her wrong.

"Nine days." He squeezed her hand and she squeezed back. "We've known each other nine days now."

"Yeah, I suppose we have. And they've been the best days. I don't want to throw in the towel over unrealistic expectations."

"Neither do I."

"So, going forward, I'd like to set some realistic ones."

"That sounds more than fair." Relief made him almost giddy.

"First, no more taking me somewhere without my consent, not by magic key or in the back of a creepy panel van."

Her eyes brightened, the dim lights of their cozy corner reflecting in their depths.

"Agreed," Dash said without hesitation.

"Second, this relationship has an expiration date. I leave two days after my sister's wedding, and I'm not ready to give up my career."

"Okay, but may I point out something?"

She nodded slowly, her brows scrunched in suspicion.

"I happen to have a magic key that can take me anywhere in the world in a single step. It's entirely possible we could come to some sort of arrangement after New Year's."

She pursed her lips and her face flushed. The idea must not have occurred to her. Dash tried to keep the smug smile suppressed, but he failed. Miserably.

Lina laughed, the musical notes of it drawing a few glances from the patrons.

"Fine. We can revisit the question. I have one more expectation." She worried her lower lip with her teeth.

"What is it, Lina? If I can, I'll do it."

Her beautiful smile lit up the dim corner, lit up his heart.

"A tour of Santa's workshop. I can't be dating Santa's son and not get a tour of the workshop."

He laughed, a big booming laugh that filled the bar with joy. The patrons turned to look. He had his father's laugh.

"Done. When?"

Lina pulled out her phone and checked her calendar. "Tomorrow? I know it's a busy time of year, but it's still a couple days before Christmas Eve."

"No problem. My dad has been doing this for so long, it's almost automatic. We have plenty of hands to pitch in, and a visitor won't be an issue. Meet me here, same time?"

"Yes, but I need to go. Dress fittings wait for no one. At least according to my mother."

She rose and tugged on her gloves. He stepped around the table and closed the distance between them. When she didn't flinch away, he cupped her cheek and kissed her, a feather-light brushing of lips against lips. Lina hummed her pleasure but stepped away before either of them could take it any further.

"I'll see you tomorrow," he said.

"I'll be here with bells on." She hurried to the exit but turned around at the last second and called across the room. "Maybe

I'll wear something else, too."

She slipped out the door, leaving him with a picture of her with nothing but bells on. Where the fuck would they go? His mind filled in so many possibilities, it left his mouth dry, his knees weak, and his cock hard.

Dash collapsed on his seat. The fates had found him a worthy match. More than worthy. He had to tell her about the helpmate bond. He'd been ready to come clean if she demanded no more secrets. But the bond would be another thing to process with the wedding and all the family events over the next week and a half. After the wedding, after New Year's, when they were negotiating magic key privileges, he would disclose it then. And pray she understood.

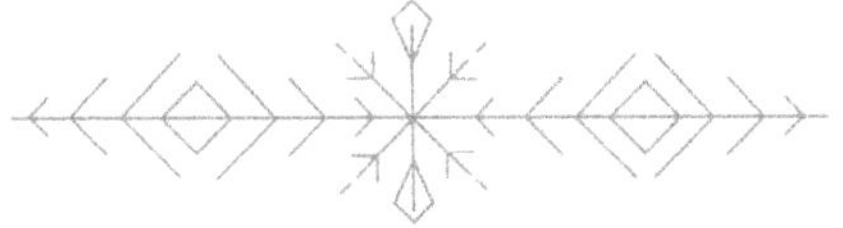

CHAPTER 18
RUDOLPH VII

Lina felt like a kid on Christmas Eve, which was a little on the nose considering she was about to see Santa's workshop up close and personal.

The sleigh bells on the door of The Old Bell announced her presence with musical joy. She stomped her boots on the mat and brushed the snow off her coat. Dash waited for her, seated on a barstool with his coat on. At least she understood why he rarely wore a hat and gloves.

He greeted her with a smile bright with delight, relief, and charm. No, not charm. Sex. Dash put so much sex in his smile it went straight to her core and the temperature of the bar rose at least ten degrees. *Shit.*

"You ready, gorgeous?" He kissed her forehead.

Well, she couldn't let that stand. "Not yet. You're forgetting something."

Delighted by the confusion she'd caused, Lina tapped her lips, giving Dash the answer he needed. A fire lit his cool blue eyes as he framed her face in his palms, running a thumb along her bottom lip. He lowered his head and kissed her, soft and sweet. He tasted of Christmas—fresh mint and new-fallen snow.

"Ready now?" he murmured in her ear, sending a low thrum of desire coursing through her blood.

"Mm-hmm." Lina was incapable of uttering anything more complex.

Dash chuckled as he took her hand and led her behind the bar. "Heading out for the day, Julia. You got what you need?"

"Sure thing, boss. Have fun!" Julia winked before Dash whisked Lina down a small hallway and into an office.

Trays on the desk held neat piles of papers, and two filing cabinets stood on the far wall. A small safe was tucked in a corner. Dash shut the cheap black door behind them with a small click. He pulled out a silvery skeleton key, the part that went into the lock shaped like a snowflake. As he held it out toward the door, a glowing keyhole appeared, and the key slid into it like…

Lina swallowed. Perhaps that wasn't the image she wanted at the moment.

The doorjamb glowed a neon blue. How in the world had she missed such radiance the other night? Dash turned the key and pushed the door open. Instead of the short, dark hallway, his bedroom stood on the other side.

"After you."

He gestured grandly, radiating holiday cheer with his sexy smile firmly affixed. Right, that was how she missed it last time—Dash had an uncanny ability to hold all her attention. Lina stepped through, and Dash followed, pocketing the key. The blue glow vanished, leaving the white door she remembered from the other night, the black door gone like a dream.

"It's that simple?" she asked.

"Yes." He slid off his coat and threw it over a chair. "Elven magic makes so many things easier. If we didn't have to hide ourselves, we could do even more good in the world."

"Why do you hide yourselves?"

She thought about it as she peeled away her layers. Magic had been long viewed as evil, not a force for good. And human beings had a poor track record dealing with events they did not understand. If the existence of elves had been widespread knowledge, they would have risked eradication.

He focused on her, a sad smile playing with the corners of his mouth. "Even under a best-case scenario, governments would study us and exploit us for what we can do and force us to do deplorable things. We've been careful about letting people, humans, know about us. It's easier to blend in and pretend we don't exist."

"What if you lose the key?" That could be disastrous—she could only imagine some child sneaking through and becoming lost in the North Pole.

"I'm the only person who can use this key. If lost, it would be just a pretty decoration. It's a pain in the ass to make another, so I try not to. But I believe I brought you here for a tour, not for a magic lesson."

Dash held out a hand and opened the door. Lina dropped her coat on the sofa and laced her fingers in his. Tingling warmth flowed from the point of contact and suffused her with peace, and some of the tension melted from his shoulders.

"So, this place is a fancy geodesic dome. The main boardroom is under the glass part, and this hallway encircles it, with the family's quarters and common areas—"

"Like the kitchen?"

"Like the kitchen. The common areas line the outside of the structure. The workshop is underneath us."

"Stables?"

"Those are outside, but there's a tunnel from the workshop, so we'll hit it last."

"Where do your workers live?"

The hall was quiet as they approached the kitchen. No one

was there, and Dash led her past it to another room. A dining room, with a long wood table the color of a perfectly toasted marshmallow. At least two dozen chairs surrounded the thing, and family portraits lined the cranberry walls above the white wainscoting.

"There are other compounds similar to this one, but smaller, scattered in a ten-kilometer radius. Geodesic domes with a few levels underneath, housing a couple hundred each."

He pointed at the portrait at the far end. Santa leaned against a red sleigh in full regalia, but his hair and beard were blond, not white, and nary a rosy cheek to be seen. Next to him stood a woman with long, wavy auburn hair. Her cheeks were rosy enough for both of them, and her smile lit the entire room. Two children played at their feet, a girl no more than four with blond curls like her dad and a boy several years older.

This was why he seemed familiar the first time they met—a family resemblance to the common archetype of Santa Claus.

"My family. My dad Ivan, my mother Katja, and my sister Joy."

"Will I meet your parents today?" She had already "met" Joy under less than ideal circumstances. She hoped they could have a real conversation someday.

"I'm not sure. Everybody is pretty busy, but if they're around, they'll take a minute to say hello."

He tugged her further along the hall until they arrived at an elevator door. It was old-fashioned, looking more like a cage than a box. Dash hit the button and the lock clicked. He pulled open the accordion-style brass gate and stepped inside the ornate elevator, pulling her in behind him. He shut everything and hit the down button. The car started with a jerk, and Lina grabbed onto Dash.

"Easy, there. It's perfectly safe," he said.

She eyed the car dubiously. "Yeah, right. How old is this

thing?"

"Granddad installed it in the late 1800s when he became Santa. There are still a few elves around who were alive then."

The elevator creaked to a stop as smooth as the start was rough.

"How long do elves live?" she asked in a small voice as he opened the gate and led her out into a small room.

Dash swallowed, and a little color left him as he answered. "About twice as long as humans."

Oh. So, if they got together, he expected to outlive her by decades. That was…sucky was the only word her mind found. But this wasn't the time to address it. This connection between them could fizzle out in a few weeks when she was back to work and his life returned to normal.

"I guess we'll have to talk about that, too. Someday."

He nodded, relief loosening the tension in his brow. Once again, he took her hand and led her to the intricately carved doors on the other side of the room. Snowflakes covered the top half of the doors, but the bottom half had a beautiful bas-relief rendition of the same sleigh from the family portrait, along with eight reindeer.

"Where's Rudolph?" she asked, joking.

"The door was carved before the first Rudolph."

"There's more than one?"

He chuckled, leaning into the *ho, ho, ho* of it all. "A few reindeer with glowing noses are born in each generation. The fastest one is dubbed Rudolph. We're up to Rudolph VII."

With a flourish, Dash opened the doors. On the other side was a cavernous space filled with worktables and conveyor belts and noise and elves. So many elves. Tall ones, short ones, fat and thin and everything between, skin and hair of all shades, each wearing protective eyewear, and those with long hair had it tied back.

Dash slowly guided her through the space, pausing wherever her gaze lingered for more than a heartbeat. There were elves painting wooden toys of all kinds. Cars, planes, boats, trains, animals. There were elves sewing button eyes onto stuffed animals. Some were incredibly realistic, but others were fantastical creations straight out of sugarplum dreams. Still more elves were boxing and wrapping the toys on long conveyor belts.

"Since we're so close to delivery, they're putting the finishing touches on some of these things. We load the sleigh tomorrow and everybody receives their schedule tonight," he explained as they moved seamlessly through the busy workshop.

"Everybody?"

"Every adult North Pole elf will have some gifts to deliver on Christmas Eve. No exceptions. Some volunteer from elsewhere, too. How else are 500 million children going to get toys for Christmas?"

That made sense, but… "Why elves?"

"I'll tell you, but you have to swear to keep the secret. No one must know, not even your family." His eyes twinkled, though, so Lina doubted he was serious.

"You have my word," she said solemnly.

"One of my ancestors was injured, and a human gave him shelter until he was well enough to travel. It was near Christmas, and great-whatever-grandpa was fascinated by the holiday. Close to, but different from, some of his own rituals around the winter solstice. To repay the kindness, my ancestor snuck gifts into the human's home each year. The mission grew until we have the enterprise you see today."

He gestured broadly at the busy elves, the conveyor belts, the worktables, all of it. They reached the far side of the factory, and a familiar figure waited behind a desk lined with monitors, the tall Black elf she'd encountered the other night. He rose as they approached.

"Hugo, this is Lina, my…guest. Hugo is the head of North Pole security."

"Lina, I'm sorry if I startled you the other night." Hugo held out his hand and she took it. He had just been doing his job. "I spend most of my time keeping the reindeer from escaping, teenagers from making out in the workshop, and escorting home the occasional elf who drank too much. It's been many years since we found a human wandering the main compound."

"No worries. I'm afraid I wasn't in the best state of mind."

Hugo shot Dash an irritated look but had nothing but a kindly smile for Lina.

"You'll find muck boots and outdoor gear at the stable. If I might offer some advice—Cupid bites. Stay as far from that nuisance as you can."

"It was one time, Hugo," Dash said, exasperation in his tone.

"One time too many, Dash. He's ready for retirement."

"Except he's as excited as all the yearlings whenever we bring out the harnesses."

"Talk to me again when you're ready for retirement." Hugo chuckled and pulled open the doors behind him, the twins to the ones on the other side of the workshop.

Dash gave him a quick salute and Lina waggled her fingers as they walked into the long, dimly lit tunnel. The lights brightened as they made their way down the corridor, and the door closed behind them.

"Magic or motion sensors?" Lina tried not to strain her neck as she looked up.

"Magic. Wiring this tunnel would be a pain in the ass. Plus, this is where we bring the reindeer when the weather turns more inhospitable than usual. Their magic doesn't do well with complex tech. A lightbulb is fine, but the motion sensors would burn out."

They walked for a couple of minutes, coming to a line of

benches. Tucked underneath were rubber boots and shoes of various kinds. Dash sat and removed his shoes. He pulled on a pair of boots. Glancing at her feet, he gestured at another pair of boots on the other side of the corridor, about halfway down.

"Those should fit."

She mimicked him, grateful she wouldn't have to worry about bringing home reindeer shit on the bottoms of her shoes. It might be a little difficult to explain.

Gee, Cassie, I guess I must have picked it up when I visited Rudolph at the North Pole.

Yeah, that would go over great. She saw Dash's point. It's hard to explain the impossible, even to someone you trust.

He pushed open a door at the end of the tunnel. These were much more utilitarian than the ones leading into the workshop, though made of the same wood. A pair of snowflakes at least five feet across decorated the doors, carved by an expert craftsperson. This door led them into a small vestibule, and Lina faced yet another entry.

"They'll try to escape into the tunnel, so we do a kind of air lock thing," Dash explained as he opened the next set of doors.

Warm, humid air greeted them as they stepped into the stable, and it smelled much like she expected a stable to smell, like all the stables she'd entered the past decade on her far-flung journeys. Hay and dirt and dung and a musky animal scent that varied subtly depending on whether pigs, horses, goats, cows, or apparently, reindeer resided.

She expected a layout similar to a horse stable, with individual stalls. Instead, it was a large space, not unlike a warehouse, with hay strewn on the floor, feeding troughs around the circumference, and a large tub of water in the middle.

A small herd of reindeer milled about. One with a bright red nose trotted straight toward them. It stopped just short of Dash and snuffled at him. Dash stroked its nose.

"And this is the current Rudolph. Come here. Let him smell you and then you can pet him, too."

She inched closer. Those antlers looked deadly, but she held out her hand. His nose and breath were warm and moist, and he nuzzled her hand. Lina relaxed and enjoyed the velvety sensation of his snout.

As though this was some sort of signal, the rest of the herd ambled over.

"Which one is Cupid?" she muttered out of the side of her mouth.

"You don't need to worry. It was only once, and Hugo hadn't been paying attention. We won't be here long enough for Cupid to get antsy."

More reindeer pressed their noses into her hand, snuffling and sniffing, one at a time, until each had greeted her in their cervid way. Lina had passed some sort of test, but whether it was of Dash's devising or the reindeer's, she had no idea.

A last reindeer remained by her side, trailing after her like a lost puppy as she slowly paced the barn.

"They're amazing," she said.

"Seems Stanley feels the same way about you." He looked away and mumbled something that sounded suspiciously like, "I do too."

"I'm sorry, I didn't catch the last bit." Lina only kept her expression neutral with a gargantuan effort. She longed to call him on it, tease him, but perhaps today wasn't the day. It had been a lot for her, too—wasn't every day she was invited to explore a magical new world.

"Do you want to go outside?"

Lina shivered. "No thank you. Boston winters are bad enough. I don't need to learn how bad Greenland can be. Another time?"

His face lit up as if she'd promised to take him to the zoo. Or take him to his bedroom for some one-on-one activities.

"I have one more place to show you. It's my favorite room in the entire compound." Dash led her to the entrance. The reindeer still followed her. He turned and pressed his hand against the animal's head. "Stay, Stanley."

The reindeer grumbled and snorted, looking longingly at Lina.

"Go on. I'll come back to visit," she said.

Another snort, but Stanley trotted away and joined the rest of the herd. Dash ushered her through the door and they put their shoes on, leaving the boots tucked under the benches as they'd found them.

He pulled out his magic key, opened a magic doorway, leading her into a round room with a glass dome. The aurora borealis shone brightly above them, swirls of green and blue and a hint of purple.

"The aurora isn't usually so bright in December," he said.

Lina tore her gaze from the show to watch the light play across his features, highlighting his rounded cheeks and reflecting in his ice-blue eyes. He truly looked like an elf in this light, in this place. Otherworldly, powerful, even a bit frightening. He turned to her, and something fierce and hot replaced the magical. This she understood. It was feral, carnal, and it was all for her.

But still he hesitated. So Lina took matters into her own hands. She had forgiven him, and it was time to prove it. She snagged his belt and pulled him close. Standing on tiptoe, she kissed him hard, demanding he kiss her back. An instant later, he answered her demand with one of his own, thrusting his tongue into her mouth.

A low moan escaped her, and he smiled as he continued to lick and nibble her quickly swelling lips.

Oh, that's how this is going to be? Two can play this game, mister.

With a quick flick of her fingers, she undid the button on his jeans and pulled down the zipper. She trailed her cool hands over his silky boxer briefs and his hard cock. His rumbling groan thrummed through her, setting her skin on fire.

Dash broke the kiss, trailing his lips along her jaw until he paused just below her earlobe.

"Do you want to know a secret?" he asked.

Of course she did. "Mm-hmm."

"I've had fantasies about fucking you on this table while you look up into the infinite sky. Would you like me to do that someday?"

Her knees went weak at the thought, and she said the only thing strong enough to fight through the fog of desire. "Is today someday?"

He crushed her to him, taking her mouth again, and hardened beneath her light touch. Damn, she craved him.

Dash lifted her, and she wrapped her legs around his waist. He cupped her ass and held her as if she weighed nothing, though that was far from true. Slowly inching toward the table, he delved his tongue in and out of her mouth. Quiet mewling escaped from her.

Someone cleared their throat.

Dash stilled and broke the kiss. Lina looked over his shoulder, and her entire body burned with embarrassment. Standing in the doorway was none other than the man himself. White hair, white beard, as tall as Dash with his rosy cheeks, and a touch of a round belly. The only thing she hadn't expected were the pointy elf ears.

Oh, and the scowl.

Chapter 19
Drinking and Flying

His dad's appearance sent ice running through his veins, instantly quenching the lust Lina sparked. Dash gently let her down, and she buried her flaming face in his chest as he zipped his pants. The scowl on Ivan Nichol's usually jolly visage was thunderous. He hadn't seen its like since Joy went to Mexico one spring break in college without informing anybody. And it hadn't been turned on Dash himself since he'd "borrowed" the sleigh the summer after he turned sixteen.

He put himself between Lina and his father, hoping she hadn't noticed the scowl. A person's first meeting with the man in the flesh shouldn't be tarnished with anger, but he feared he was too late.

"Hi, Dad."

"Dash. Why have you brought a human here?"

"This is Lina. I owed her a tour of the place."

"Owed?"

"Yeah, I fucked up her first visit."

"Language." His mother's voice came from just out of sight.

She stepped into the room a moment later, and his father's scowl softened as he wrapped an arm around Katja.

Dash stepped to the side. "Lina, this is my dad Ivan, the current Santa Claus, and my mom Katja."

Lina tugged on her sweater, straightened her shoulders, and Dash could almost hear her thinking, *Fuck it.*

Walking the few feet separating them, Lina stuck out her hand and plastered on a seemingly genuine smile. "Nice to meet you, sir, ma'am."

His dad went into full-on Santa mode. A jolly smile replaced what remained of the scowl, and his eyes twinkled like the stars in a clear midnight sky in the depths of winter. He took Lina's hand and shook it vigorously.

"Ho, ho, ho, the pleasure is all mine, Carolina. Any friend of my son is most welcome."

Lina blinked. "How—"

His dad tapped the side of his nose and winked. Lina shut her mouth and shook her head. Apparently, his dad was going with the "pretend nothing happened" option for these types of situations. If this had happened when Dash was in his twenties, it would be the "are you out of your mind" lecture option. But he was nearly forty, and to suggest Dash wasn't capable of making his own decisions would be disingenuous at best.

His mother examined Lina head to toe, and a sly grin formed. When Lina turned to shake her hand, his mom pulled her in for a quick hug. Oh, boy.

But Lina didn't appear taken aback, or at least she hid it well. She returned the hug, before stepping away.

"So, how was the tour? Did Dash take you to meet the reindeer?" Katja asked.

Dash lost track of the conversation as Lina's eyes brightened. They drew him in and shut out the rest of the world. He would happily forget everything else and live for the moments when Lina's eyes shone like fairy lights in a deep forest. They were hypnotic. Or he was truly smitten. Or the helpmate bond *really* fucked with his head.

The silence brought him out of his fugue state. Both his parents and Lina were staring at him.

"I missed something," Dash said.

Lina's lips quirked up, but the hint of a scowl returned to his father's brow.

"Your dad asked when you were taking me back," she said.

"Ah, now-ish. I know you have things to do." Dash stuck his hands in his pockets. Thank god his father's voice was an instant boner killer.

"As do we." His dad gave Dash a meaningful look.

Shit, this wasn't the end of the conversation. Guess he was getting the lecture anyway.

"It was nice meeting you." Some of Lina's joy disappeared as she read the room.

"Have a very merry Christmas, Lina," Ivan said before walking into the hall.

"The pleasure was all ours." Katja frowned at Ivan's back. "And don't worry too much about my husband. The stress of the season makes him a tad grumpy."

"I am not grumpy, woman!" Ivan's voice echoed in the hall, and Katja grinned before disappearing after him.

Dash raked his gaze over Lina, beyond disappointed their sexy times session needed to be postponed. But she had her sister's wedding hanging over her, and he had Christmas. He plastered on a smile that was more wooden than he wished.

"Ready?"

"No," she sighed. "But I guess it's time."

He snagged her around the waist and brought her in close. Planting a kiss on her forehead, he inhaled. Her spicy cinnamon scent was strongest in her hair. He could wrap it around him and be happy for the rest of his long, long days.

"After the holiday, it's entirely different around here for a few weeks. Nobody does anything until at least February except read and eat. Let me take you home."

He slipped his hand down and entangled their fingers. Leading her to his room, Dash tried not to let the depressing cloud dampen her mood. He helped her with her jacket and watched as she pulled the boring old hat over her dark curls. Her granny hat made a significant difference. She had looked exuberant and ready to take on the world with her colorful monstrosity. This one…it sucked the rosiness from her cheeks and the delight from her eyes.

The idea he'd had about finding her hat nudged him again. He should do something about it.

Dash cupped her cheek and kissed her gently. And kept it brief. No need to incur his father's wrath by being late to his lecture about trying to seduce beautiful women in the boardroom.

"I'll call you tomorrow," he said, pulling out the key.

"You better. I need to make sure this was real and not some delusion."

"Oh, it's real. *All* of it." He opened the gateway to the hall outside her condo.

She stepped through and looked over her shoulder with a sultry smile. "Goodnight, Dash."

When the portal closed, he went to find his father in his study. All the best lectures took place in Santa's study. The one about misusing the North Pole keys. The one about drinking and flying. The one about the proper use of condoms and other forms of birth control.

Dash pushed open the door. His father was sitting behind his desk, as expected. But what he hadn't expected were his mother and sister in the leather chairs to the side. Great, a family meeting. He was too old for this.

"Before you say you're too old for an intervention, hear us

out," his dad said, either reading his mind or his expression.

He could fight it, but they'd only choose another date and place, and during their busy season that wasted everybody's precious time. Although he didn't want to be part of the family business, he was still respectful of their needs.

He sat in the uncomfortable wooden chair in front of his father's desk, the one that made you sit straighter so you didn't end up with a bruise on your tailbone from the hard-as-a-rock seat. But the conversation began on an unexpected note.

"Tell me about Lina," his dad said, more kindly than any previous lecture.

"What do you want to know?" Was he ready to drop the big bomb? A human as helpmate to the son of Ivan Nichols could go over worse than a lump of coal on Christmas Day.

"How did you meet?"

Dash glanced at his mother. She was doing the thing. The thing with her face that she always did when she knew a secret and wanted to spill her guts but wouldn't. It was only a matter of time before his dad took note and had every detail from her. The only reason he hadn't noticed yet was the rush of the Christmas season.

"She came to The Old Bell. We, uh, hit it off."

"I understand this isn't her first trip here. Why wasn't I informed of either visit?"

"You've never wanted to be informed when we have a special visitor, and you're busy right now. The first visit was a bit of a…mess. This time was to make up for the mistake."

"But she's human, Dash. That's different, especially after Victoria. Not to mention, there's the difference in life expectancy. And what about kids? You know elves and humans often have difficulty conceiving. Who will inherit the mantle of Santa Claus?"

"Hey, you have two kids," Joy said, finally speaking. "It's not all about Dash."

"Your father knows that," his mother said, "but you're not rushing to find a significant other yet."

Joy glowered at their parents, crossing her arms defensively.

"Why are you jumping to so many conclusions?" Dash said. "We won't be the first elf-human couple in recent memory. Surely, we can find some magical solution to the life expectancy issue, and we haven't even talked about kids yet. We've known each other days."

"Days? And you already told her our secrets? What were you thinking?"

There it was; the old standby. Dash opened his mouth to reply, but his mother beat him to it.

"Ivan, enough. He's not a child, and I trust he knows what he's doing." This time, his mother's face told a different story—he'd better know what he was doing, or his father would be the least of his worries. "Dash will deal with the consequences one way or another."

"I don't like it. He's rushing into this, and it doesn't affect only him. His little human could put the entire elven community in danger. And for what? A tumble—"

Dash slapped the desk. "Don't complete that sentence, Dad. I'd hate for either of us to say something we'd regret."

Some of the wind left his dad's sails. Ivan crossed his arms and looked as if he wanted to argue. Joy and he were a matched set, filled with barely contained irritation. But his dad was a smart man and kept his mouth shut.

"You need to proceed carefully, Dash." His mother broke the tense silence. "For your sake and hers."

He nodded, and sympathy flashed in her eyes.

"Fine," his dad said, standing. "But if there's a pile of reindeer droppings left if things go south, I am *not* picking up a shovel."

"Great. I can handle a shovel all by myself." Dash wished he sounded like anything other than a petulant teen.

"I'm off to prep for tomorrow. Goodnight."

His father left the room, his steps thudding down the hall. Katja rose and gripped Dash's shoulder briefly.

"You need to tell him, sooner rather than later," she whispered before following her husband.

"Well, that was interesting." Joy inflected all the younger sibling annoyance she could into the simple sentence.

"I thought you'd fallen asleep. You're not usually so…restrained when I get reamed a new asshole."

"Just sitting back and enjoying the show. Not often the golden child gets his ass handed to him." She propped her legs on their dad's desk and put her hands behind her head, as though she hadn't a care in the world.

"I'm the golden child? You're the one following him around like a shadow. You're the one who dreams of running this enterprise when he's ready to hand over the reins. Not me."

"That's what pisses me off the most. Dad assumes you're going to take over just because of the junk between your legs. It's old-fashioned and gross."

Joy was right. Although Dash had shown little interest in North Pole Enterprises, his parents, especially his dad, assumed he would take over. But Dash had his own plans. The restaurant business was far more interesting to him than toys. He'd enjoyed making toys, wrapping them, and delivering them on Christmas Eve as a child and young adult, but the day-to-day logistics of running the North Pole left him, well, cold.

"What do you want me to do, Joy?"

"Talk to them, talk to *him*. Make Dad realize I'm the best person for the job. Bring him into the 21st century. Hell, any of the older elves could drive the sleigh on Christmas Eve and play the part. Even you could do it with a bit of glamour. Then I could do what I do best and make sure everything runs smoothly."

His sister, despite her annoying habit of being right far too often, deserved the job. And, frankly, driving the sleigh on the big night would be the perfect task for him. He loved delivering gifts, loved the reindeer, and the sleigh handled like a race car. They both could have what they wanted.

"I'll do it, I promise."

"When?"

"By the end of January. Christmas will be over, and whatever is going to happen with Lina will have settled."

Joy's blue eyes, near twins to his, grew as big as sugar cookies, and she dropped her casual act, leaning forward.

"Swear it."

"No."

"Swear it or I'll hide all the shovels when it's your turn to muck the stables."

She would do it too, the brat.

"Fine. I swear on sleigh bells, red ribbons, and Rudolph's nose I will tell our father before February I have no intention of running the North Pole and you, my baby sister and thorn in my ass, are the best possible candidate to succeed him when he retires."

She stuck her tongue out at him, but her hostility melted away.

"Good. Now, what are you getting this woman of yours for Christmas? It's only a few days away."

"We've been dating less than two weeks."

Joy smiled, a sly thing that slithered across her face like a serpent bent on hunting down a sinner. "Uh-huh. You got yourself a sticky candy cane there. Get her nothing and it appears you don't care at all. Get her something too personal and it appears you're ready to look for a ring next week."

His palms grew sweaty and the room suddenly was too hot.

He hated how right she was. How the fuck had Joy gotten so smart?

An idea knocked on the inside of his skull. It could work. Personal enough to say he cared, but not enough to scare Lina off.

"Actually…what do you know about spells for finding things?"

Chapter 20
On the Naughty List

Each time Lina's phone dinged at her the next day, her heart leaped, her palms sweated, and snowflakes did somersaults in her stomach. And each time, it wasn't him.

The wedding planner messaged her five times, trying to finalize everything before Christmas. Each bridesmaid had a different question about when and where to meet for hair, nails, and makeup. She received three calls from her parents, two from her mom and a butt-dial from her dad. And the florist nearly caused her to have a heart attack when he called to say the flowers wouldn't be in, only to realize that, A, he was supposed to call the wedding planner, and B, it was a different event.

All this while running around the wintry Boston streets trying to finish her Christmas shopping, wrapping the gifts, and putting them under the small tree Wes and Cassie had set up. Though she'd brought some souvenirs for her family, she kept busy buying the more substantial gifts from shops around Boston.

Lina found a beautiful silk scarf for her mother from a museum gift shop, the newest hardback books by a couple of her dad's favorite authors, and a pretty pair of earrings from a boutique Cassie loved. Wesley was harder, but she had planned his gift months ago and recruited Tiên to help. She paired their ridiculous treasure with a few sci-fi paperbacks, which would be easy to slip into his briefcase for the rare down moment.

Lina had mailed the souvenirs she bought for her uncle and cousins a few days after arriving in Boston, so they were done. And she'd given Tiên a framed photo of the Parthenon when they met for lunch. Her friend swore she would travel someday, but for now she lived vicariously through Lina's experiences.

While Lina enjoyed the brisk December air turning her nose red, and the warm to-go cups of peppermint mochas from Dunks, she missed her cozy hat. Cassie's backup navy one didn't put a spring in her step. Not to mention, she always hatched the most imaginative ideas while wearing her granny hat and boy, did she need an excellent idea.

The only person she couldn't find a gift for was Dash. What did you buy for a man you've known for less than two weeks, gone on three dates with—did the tour of the North Pole count as a date? If so, make that four dates—and spent the night with once? What did you buy for a man who may not be in your life for more than another ten days? Almost anything seemed too much, and yet not acknowledging it at all seemed weird. Especially since the man was the son of Santa Claus. Surely, Christmas gifts were an art form in his family. Should she even bother trying?

You could ask him, a tiny voice murmured in the back of her mind. Her logical, socially competent conscience.

She could, perhaps she should, but he might assume she was fishing for a gift. Would she be? Hell, who knew anymore? This whole dating Santa's son was more confusing than she imagined when she decided to give him a second chance. There was the secrecy, there was the magic, and there was the fact she would die long before him. How could she be enough when he was looking at decades of loneliness after her death?

As she passed a small shop outside the T stop by the condo, an item caught her eye, something that drove away the melancholy her thoughts had draped over her. It would be perfect. She darted in, just before closing, and made her purchase. Lina hurried to her sister's place, nearly giggling the whole way there.

She wrapped it and placed it with the rest of the gifts under the tree. Cassie and Wes were dining with both sets of parents tonight. Lina had demurred, wishing for a quiet evening before the chaos of the holiday and the wedding overwhelmed everything else in her life. She poured herself a glass of wine and collapsed on the couch.

And yet, still no call from Dash. Or a text. Not even a "got busy, will try tomorrow."

She believed yesterday had gone well, even though none other than the big guy himself had interrupted them. Lina doubted she could ever live it down. Holy crap, making out with Santa's son surely would land her on the naughty list. If Dash ever called, she would ask.

Lina poured another glass, grabbed some cheese and crackers, and watched a wicked hokey holiday movie. Despite her best efforts, she ended up needing the tissues her sister had left on the coffee table knowing Lina's predilection for sappy Christmas fare.

She checked her phone—nothing. Hopefully, he had a good reason.

Washing her plate and glass, Lina decided to head to bed. No reason to get her panties in a twist. Dash was a busy man, and this was a particularly busy time of year for him. He would call when he had a chance.

She slipped into her flannel pajamas and slid under the covers, grabbing the book she'd abandoned earlier from the nightstand.

The phone rang.

"It's about time. I'm already in bed," she said sweetly. No need to clue him in she'd almost given up.

"Hey, Lina." His voice flowed over her, warm and sweet and earthy, like the best hot cocoa. It melted her insides and dampened her panties. "I'm sorry. My backup bartender called in sick, and the ice machine broke. I managed to sneak away for a few minutes, but it won't be long before somebody needs me."

"I won't keep you. I appreciate—"

"No, you're not getting rid of me so easy. I've been looking forward to this all damn day."

"Talking to me?"

"Yes, talking to you. I'd hoped we'd be able to do…more, but work got in the way."

The way he purred "more" thrummed through her, striking all the right chords deep in her core. Lina bit her lip and rubbed her thighs together, trying hard not to imagine what he meant by that. It wouldn't do much good, anyway, on opposite ends of a phone call.

"You're a busy man, Dash. A restaurant empire to run, toys to deliver, who knows what else elves get up to this time of year."

"I'm not too busy for you, Lina. Never." He said it with such conviction, she believed it. "And I can tell you what else elves get up to."

His baritone dipped even lower, caressing her through the line. Lina shivered in delight. If he was here, she would be begging him to touch her.

"Oh?" was all she said, her naughty fantasies pushing away anything more complex.

He chuckled as though he could read her mind. "Oh yes, and they're not stories fit for children. Are you sure you want to know, Lina?"

"Yes," she breathed as her heart raced.

There was a pause and a creak, then the soft snick of a lock turning.

"We fuck like horny little lemmings. We get all cozy with a willing partner, or the lucky ones with a significant other, pile on the blankets, and spend hours giving and receiving pleasure."

The image his words conjured, the tone of his voice, her desperate desire for this man all took her words away. She panted softly into the phone, scrambling for something to say. Dash saved her the trouble.

"I don't have hours, but maybe we can scratch this itch. Are you in?"

"Yes," she said without hesitation, and she meant it. Ever since she had met this man, she wanted him. His voice turned her to mush, and his hands worked wonders. She was in—all in.

"Excellent." Another creak, followed by the soft metallic slide of a zipper. "Hearing your voice, imagining you in bed, I'm so hard. Tell me you're wet for me."

Lina licked her lips. She was doing this. Phone sex. Despite her history of failed long-distance relationships, none had advanced to the phone sex phase. Oh hot damn, she was having phone sex with Dash.

"I am. So wet. Your voice…it's like you're stroking me from the inside."

Another rumble over the line, and once again she pressed her thighs together. If she was doing this, she wanted it to last.

"Rub your nipple for me, Lina. Your noises are mine, don't you dare keep them from me."

She slid her hand under her top and did as he demanded, letting out a small gasp.

"Again," he ordered roughly.

She did it again, and a low moan slipped from her lips.

"Dash." It was a plea, but she didn't know for what.

"You want more." Not a question. "Run your fingers down

your body and touch your pussy for me."

She did exactly as he said, imagining the whole time her fingers were his. Wishing they were his. And when she touched her pussy, it was almost as though it was Dash. Her moan would have been embarrassing, but she was beyond being embarrassed. She needed him, however she could have him.

The idea both thrilled her and frightened her out of her wits. This was supposed to be a fling, yet it felt anything but.

"I'm so hard for you. I wish your hand was wrapped around my cock. Do you wish it was your hand?"

"Yes, I want it to be my hand. I want to stroke you, and lick you, make you come."

"Fuuck. Put your fingers in your pussy."

They slid right in, she was so wet.

"Now, rub your clit for me, angel."

Lina panted as the tension wound tight inside her, the occasional moan escaping. She was lost to anything other than the pleasure and his voice in her ear.

"I want you, Dash. I want your cock in my pussy."

"Soon, Lina, soon. I'm so close. Are you close?"

She was so, so close. The smallest push would send her over the edge.

"Yes."

The sounds of his hand on his cock came through the phone.

"Come for me," he demanded.

She rubbed her clit one last time before shattering, a long sob filling the room. His groan mingled with it as he came. Lina slowly floated back into her own body, her cheeks flushing at what she had done.

Lina laughed. It started as a satisfied chuckle, then morphed into outright laughter.

"What's funny?" Dash rumbled.

A jolt of uncertainty struck her. She'd never had any

complaints in bed, but…

"I've never done that before. Was it—was I…good?"

"Seemed like you enjoyed yourself. God knows I did. I'd call that good."

The slight noise from his zipper came through the phone.

"Thank you, Dash." She had no idea what else to say. Thanks for the best phone sex of my life? Thanks for the *only* phone sex of my life? Thanks for the orgasm?

"Anytime, Lina. Literally, anytime. I don't do that very often, but I can't get enough of you."

A knock sounded on his end of the line.

"Give me five!" It was muffled, as though he'd covered the microphone. "I'm sorry—"

"You've got to go. I understand."

"I don't want you to think I called you just to get off."

Though the thought hadn't crossed her mind, it was nice to hear the words. "I don't. It was a lovely bonus, though. Goodnight, Dash."

"Goodnight, Lina. Sleep well."

The line went dead, and Lina slept like a baby.

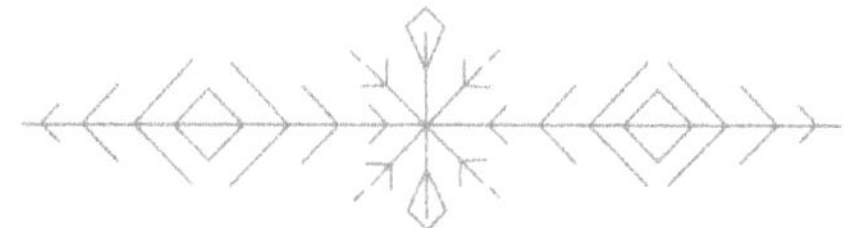

CHAPTER 21
THERE'S ALWAYS FLOWERS

He bought the extra fancy candles, smudged the crap out of his room with lavender and cedar, and called upon the winds to help him find Lina's hat. Hell, he even sent a prayer out to Saint Anthony, just in case.

Nothing. Magic wasn't his area of expertise. He had it, he could use it, he sometimes did, but when he needed it to work the most, all he got were crickets.

Abandoning the spell for the night, he went to the dining room, where they kept the liquor. He poured a hefty measure of good Kentucky bourbon and sat, propping his feet on the table. Christmas was less than thirty-six hours away, and he would be busy all Christmas Eve delivering gifts. Fuck, what was he going to get Lina with less than twelve hours to plan and shop?

"Mom will kill you for putting your dirty-ass boots on her heirloom dining table." Joy sauntered in and helped herself to a flavored vodka. She joined him, propping her own slippered feet on the table.

"What's good for the gander…" He gestured at her own apparent lack of respect for an old table.

"My dude, these are my house slippers. Who knows where

your boots have been? On the sticky floor behind your bar, I bet. Ew."

She had a point. He pulled off the boots and set them on the floor.

"That's not any better." Joy scooted over one chair, disgust wrinkling her nose.

"The spell didn't work, oh font of magical knowledge, and I don't have a backup gift." He glared at his sister over the rim of his crystal glass.

"Sucks to be you." She downed her vodka and poured another.

"Lina's special, Joy, and her hat is special. Got any other tips for me?"

She considered him, and for a moment, it appeared she wished to spout off another sarcastic and useless remark. But his sister surprised him.

"If you had a thread from the original object, I'd give your odds at ninety percent." Joy studied her glass, refusing to meet his gaze. "The hat must be loaded with her DNA, so if you had a sample and could rule out where she was, where her family was, it might ping. Fifty-fifty."

He had neither of those things. He could ask Lina, but that would spoil the surprise. He needed another idea, stat.

Joy finally looked at him, a sly smile on her lips. "There's always flowers. Chocolates. Promises—"

"Shut up." He finished his bourbon and debated pouring another.

Wait a minute. What did the Beast end up giving Belle? Access to his library. What did Dash have? Access to portals anywhere on Earth. And a shit ton of gifts to give to children all over the world. What did Lina want besides her hat? To help people.

"Joy, you are a fucking genius."

She watched him warily. "Yes, *I* know that, but why do *you* suddenly think so?"

"I'm going to give Lina the best Christmas Eve of her life!"

Realization dawned on his sister's sweet face. "Oh no."

"Oh yes."

"Dad—"

"Doesn't have to know. And even if he finds out, the cat is already out of the bag, and we can always do with an extra pair of hands on Christmas Eve."

Arguing with his father with the big night looming would be counterproductive. Besides, with the last-minute snafus, all the deliveries, and general chaos, Ivan would probably never notice. Not to mention his dad would be on board once he found out about the helpmate bond. Of course, Dash would have to tell Lina about the bond, too, and…

He hated his cowardice, but she was so important to him, he couldn't risk losing her until he had no other choice.

"He's gonna shit a sleigh bell."

Dash couldn't keep the Grinchy grin in check. "I know."

"Your funeral. I'll make sure to dry clean my best black dress."

He stood and strode to the hall. "You do that. See you in a few hours."

Dash took the glass to the kitchen, washed it, and planned his surprise for Lina.

He texted her right away, telling her to be ready at noon the next day for a special Christmas surprise. Then he went to bed. Tomorrow was the big day—by the time he woke in the wee hours of the morning, it would already be evening on the other side of the world. And Christmas waited for nobody, not even Santa's son.

At precisely noon Boston time on Christmas Eve, Dash opened a portal into Lina's hall. He knocked on the condo's door, and Lina opened it almost immediately. Cassie and her fiancé were nowhere to be seen.

"Hi, nice hat." Lina's gaze caught on the stereotypical red Santa hat on his head. It was of much better quality than most. Red cashmere with a bleached wool band and pom, lined with red silk. "Do you want to come in for a drink? We have some wassail."

"No, I'm afraid not. Tight schedule, and we can't be late. Here, I got you this."

He presented her a matching hat, and her eyes widened while a slow smile spread across her face. "I love it! Thank you so much."

She put it on and delight lit her up like a Christmas tree.

"It's not your granny hat, but it comes straight from the North Pole."

"It's very sweet of you. I know you're busy, so thanks for stopping by."

Lina stood on tiptoe and kissed his cheek. He turned and caught her lips with his own. There wasn't time to explore, but a soft hum escaped her as their lips parted.

"That's not all, Lina." He threaded his fingers through hers.

"Oh?"

"Want to go on an adventure? We could use help delivering Christmas gifts."

She froze under his touch. "You…want me to help deliver Christmas presents? With the elves?"

"Yes!"

"Can we ride in the sleigh?"

"Not this time." He preferred to keep her far away from the sleigh, because otherwise his father would find out what they were doing. "But I've got a pile of presents in the workshop that need new homes. What do you say, Carolina Schultz? Care to work your way onto the 'nice' list?"

He held out his hand, hope warming him. She took it.

"Ho, ho, ho, let's go!" Lina pulled him into the condo and wrapped her arms behind his neck, kissing him for all she was worth.

Dash almost forgot they had a mission, so lost in the feel of her, the smell of her, the taste of her. But she pulled away, bouncing on her toes.

"I have a gift for you, too. Wait here." She hurried to the small tree in the living room and grabbed a box wrapped in gold paper and adorned with red ribbons. Lina returned faster than Rudolf could run. "Okay, I'm ready."

He took the key from his pocket and opened the portal to his home. Someday, hopefully soon, it would be hers too.

She gave him the gift as soon as the portal closed. "You said we're on a tight schedule, so you don't have to unwrap it right—"

Dash covered her lips with a finger. "There's always time for Christmas presents."

At her wide smile, he tore into the wrapping paper and opened the box. Nestled inside some white tissue paper was a red fuzzy blanket with a picture of a cat in a Christmas tree, all tangled in the lights. In flowing black script was written, *On the naughty list. I regret nothing.*

Dash let out a booming laugh and hugged her tightly. It perfectly encapsulated their whirlwind romance. He was tangled up in her, and he didn't regret it one bit.

"I love it! I guess this means you're not on the naughty list anymore."

Lina pushed her chest into his and danced her fingers up his side. "I could be," she purred.

He kissed her again, fiercely but all too briefly.

"We really have to go." He put the box on the bed and grabbed her hand.

They hurried along the hall, into the creaky, wondrous old elevator, then the distribution center, located below the workshop. Dozens of doorways lined the walls and wrapped gifts rested on miles of shelves. The doors all glowed icy blue and hundreds of elves passed back and forth, grabbing packages and rushing through the doors to deliver cheer on Christmas Eve.

Dash dragged her to a set of shelves near the last unlit doorway.

"We've got our own." He once again pulled out the magic key.

"I thought you had to have been there," Lina said, but grabbed a gift anyway.

"Rules are different on Christmas. Magic is tied to intention, and the intention is to deliver the gifts to the children. Somehow, it works. You can ask my sister if you want more. She's much better at magical theory than I am. You know, how tech geeks can explain how your computer or your phone works, but you're just happy it does?"

She chuckled, clutching a green-wrapped package close. "So, how do we do this?"

He pulled two large sacks off the end of the shelf and gave one to her. "Fill this, then we go through the door to deliver the gifts. We repeat until our shelf is clear."

Lina regarded the very tall, very wide, very long shelf dubiously. "Oh, yes, until it's clear."

"Don't worry. It goes faster than you think. Time's a-wasting."

Dash swept his arm and filled his bag. There were more gifts in there than she might assume would fit. Lina noticed this as well, and her face shimmered with glee.

"Please tell me this is bigger on the inside. Please, please, please." Once again, she bounced on her toes with excitement.

"It's bigger on the inside."

She squealed as she loaded as many gifts as she could into it. He clasped her hand and led her to the door. The magic key came out again and the doorway glowed. He turned the key in the lock that appeared and they stepped through.

It was a hospital somewhere on the other side of the world. From the walls decorated with kangaroos, koalas, kookaburras, and crocodiles, he was going to assume Australia. The gifts belonging here came to hand by whatever magic controlled these things, and they made a lovely, festive pile under the Christmas tree set up in the common room.

They popped back through and went to another hospital. Then a group home for teenagers. Then a few residences.

Lina giggled and oohed and ahhed, and every once in a while, her hand found his. Her touch thrilled him, and he would love doing this with her every year for the rest of his life.

Lina deserved to know she was his helpmate and he was hers. Tonight, when the deliveries were done, he would reveal all, wedding be damned. He needed to know her reaction before he planned out all his remaining years with her.

Hours passed. They took short cocoa breaks, but Lina was more than game to keep going. Her face was flushed, but her smile never left. She was radiant in her joy, the very picture of the Christmas spirit. His heart grew well over three sizes with happiness.

The rich musical sound of sleigh bells filled the air. Crap, was it that late already? Dash glanced at his watch. Nearly six, and time to reload the sleigh. He had planned to have Lina home an hour ago, well before his father returned for more gifts, but her delight had been infectious and the hours had slipped away. Perhaps he could escort Lina out before his father noticed her. He wanted to avoid an argument about her, especially on Christmas Eve.

But her expression halted him in his tracks. She would never forgive him if he whisked her away before she saw the whole shebang. Sleigh, reindeer, and Santa himself. He could keep her hidden, try to take her home as soon as his father landed. If he timed it right, it should work.

A small voice in the back of his mind piped up. *You could just tell her. Tell your dad, too, while you're at it. That would solve everything.*

He let fear get the best of him and kept his mouth shut.

The bay doors whooshed open, letting in the frigid arctic air. A reindeer with a nose glowing bright red flew through the opening, followed by eight more reindeer and the shiny red sleigh. Gripping the reins, his father let out a booming, "Ho, ho, ho!"

And immediately, Santa's gaze zeroed in on Lina.

Dash was screwed.

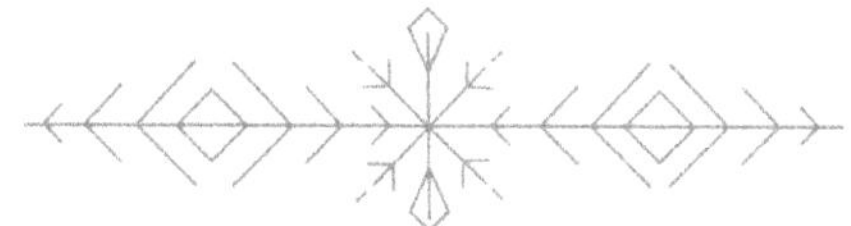

CHAPTER 22
YES–NO–IT'S COMPLICATED

A thrill of child-like awe traveled through her as Santa flew into the distribution center. It was all there, the flying reindeer, the bright sleigh, the tinkling bells, even the signature laugh. Golden sparkles flew from the sleigh's runners and the nose on the lead reindeer glowed brighter than the moon. Ivan's gaze caught hers, and the twinkling that should have been there…was not.

Lina's heart fell. Santa Claus was unhappy, possibly with her.

The sleigh landed in the clear area in the middle of the warehouse floor, hovering before slowly floating to touch down. Ivan Nichols leaped out as though he were barely older than his son. He marched over, but his smile rang false.

"Merry Christmas, Lina!" he said with a phony heartiness, holding out his hand.

She shook it, her stomach joining her heart. "Merry Christmas, Ivan."

"Can I have a moment with my son?"

"Dad, Lina—" Dash began.

"Of course. I was about ready for a break." Lina scurried down the hall to the bathroom.

She wasn't ready for a break, and she didn't want to hide in the bathroom, but there was nowhere else to go to give them privacy. Nowhere else she could hide from all the curious heads turned their way.

Splashing water on her face, she wondered what might cause Santa Claus to look as if he had dyspepsia on Christmas Eve. Lina tried to drown out the voice screaming it was her. There were other things it could be, right? One of the reindeer could be underperforming. Perhaps some gifts had been mislabeled, or he needed a cup of cocoa. Oh please, don't let it be her.

A small group of elvish women entered, chattering, but they quieted upon recognizing her, and their gazes refused to meet hers. Shit, it *was* her.

Lina trudged out and dragged her ass to the distribution center. Best to face the music sooner rather than later. It wasn't going to hurt less if Santa was displeased she showed up tonight. She must not be good enough for the heir to the family business. Of course she wasn't. She was human, and compared to Katja...

No, Lina refused to compare herself to any woman, fat, thin, or in between. She had spent her teen years doing just that, and more years of therapy unlearning it. It was fine if Ivan Nichols thought she was too fat. She didn't, and Dash certainly didn't. He hadn't suggested it once. And if he had, well, it would prove she could do better.

Though how she could do better than Dash Nichols was a mystery she hoped she would never have to solve. She'd wanted a fling, but she found him to be relationship material, despite keeping the truth about his family from her. Understandable, given the circumstances.

Or was there something more to it?

She approached the entrance, and Ivan's voice reached her.

"It turned out dreadfully for the last human you told our

secret to," he said.

"Lina isn't Victoria." Anger sharpened Dash's words.

Who the fuck was Victoria? And he had told her his secret? So much for being special. Lina had to find out herself, while Dash had the grace to tell this Victoria person.

"Who's to say? It wasn't obvious at first that Victoria had difficulty accepting the truth. If I recall correctly, it was a couple weeks later, and this human has only known, what, a few days? I don't want to wipe the memories of another human. It's dangerous."

Wipe her memories? She wouldn't remember Dash, or the North Pole, or—

The world grayed as she fought the despair welling in her gut. Lina leaned against the wall, silent and still, waiting for the other shoe to drop.

"Lina's my helpmate, Dad. Victoria wasn't. We're destined to be together."

"Your…helpmate? A human is your helpmate? That's—"

Helpmate sounded less like a prize to be won than a burden to be borne.

"Unusual, but not unheard of. It will be fine."

"What will be fine?" Lina finally found the courage to announce herself and demand answers. She pushed away from the wall and stormed into the warehouse. "And what in the hell is a helpmate?"

Dash blanched, and Ivan clenched his jaw.

"This is quite the Christmas pickle, Dash. You explain it and do what you must to fix it. I have work to do. Lina, it was good to see you, and I'm sorry my son dragged you into this."

He strode to his reloaded sleigh. He climbed in with another hearty laugh. But Lina didn't watch him fly out of sight. She poked Dash in the chest, trying to pierce through the anger coloring her vision.

"Are you going to answer me?"

Dash rubbed the back of his neck and his cheeks flushed. "Lina, I swear I planned to tell you right after your sister's wedding. You have a lot on your plate, and I didn't want to add one more thing for you to worry about."

"That doesn't explain anything. What the fuck is a helpmate?"

He clutched her arm and led her into the hall, but not far. Just enough so it would be hard to overhear them.

"It's kind of like a soulmate, I guess." He wouldn't meet her gaze.

Dash Nichols believed she was his soulmate. A woman too concerned with her career to hold a man's attention longer than a few weeks. A woman only good enough for flings. She wasn't soulmate material.

"Fated mates? You believe we're fated to be together, like God Himself joined our souls before either of us was born?"

She had never held stock in soulmates. Her parents were too logical, and she never particularly enjoyed the trope in romance novels. It was too neat, too easy.

He finally looked at her again, his blue eyes brimming with hope, with fear, and with…faith?

"Yes, but maybe not God. My ancestors believed in the Norns, the goddesses of fate."

Goddesses of fate? He was basing their entire relationship, such as it was, on predestination. He didn't love her, just thought she belonged to him. Once again, she wasn't enough. For him to love her, fate had to intervene.

"So that's why you're attracted to me? That's why you brought me here? Fate?"

The brittleness in her voice put an edge of doubt into his faithful eyes.

"Yes—no—it's complicated."

"It's not like I can go anywhere." Lina gestured around her. If she tried to leave, it was a helluva walk back to Boston. There was time to convince her he didn't assume he had a *right* to her, and he wanted her for who she was. "Uncomplicate it."

"You meet somebody, and you *know*. Not every elf is destined to find their helpmate, but many do."

That wasn't helpful, not even a little, and did nothing to dispel the growing dread settling in her stomach. By some unfathomable process, only fate had a say in the matter, not her.

"What happens if you believe you've found them, then the real one turns up?" Her voice grew smaller. What if Dash was wrong? Or worse yet, what if he was lying to take advantage of her?

"That's never happened." He seemed so sure. But could she bet her life, her heart, on a ridiculous romance trope?

"What happens in fifty years and I die of old age, and you still have decades to live on?"

He shook his head and muttered, "I don't know, but—"

"I don't believe in fate. My parents work hard at their relationship."

Wicked smart Lina Schultz, do-gooder extraordinaire, fated to be with the son of Santa Claus. It sounded like a fairy tale at best, a bad joke at worst, and minimized how much effort it took to build a real relationship, one that could truly stand the test of time, as her parents had. One day, one year, and one decade at a time, filled with love and laughter, anger and misunderstandings.

"But we won't have to."

Lina pressed her lips together. She didn't know what to think about that. She didn't know what to think about any of this. If he was trying to get something from her, she had no idea what it might be. He hadn't ditched her after sex, and a funny fuzzy Christmas blanket wasn't exactly riches untold.

"So, what you're telling me is the only reason you're attracted to me, the only reason you asked me out, is because your fates have designed me as the perfect mate for you? That what I want doesn't matter, as long as you get what you want?"

"No, that's not what I mean." He ran a hand through his hair, tugging hard. For a second, she wished he would tug harder, cause himself the same pain he caused her. "I'm not explaining this right."

"Then tell me what you mean." Some small part of her held out hope he wanted her for her, not for what he believed fate had in store.

"The helpmate bond is sacred and strong. If you don't accept it, I'll be alone for the rest of my life."

He didn't want to be alone. A fissure opened in her heart. He didn't like her for who she was, she was merely the alternative to loneliness.

Lina's alarm bells rang loud and clear, begging her to run fast and far. She told herself she refused to be someone's plan B, even if that someone was a hot bartender who could bring her to her knees with a simple look from his twinkling blue eyes. But deep down, a small voice suggested perhaps she was, in fact, afraid. Afraid of loving this man, afraid of being loved by him. So, she held tight to her anger and ignored the fear.

"I am not staying with you just so you're not lonely. That is a horrible idea. Do you know how many people suffer in bad relationships because they're afraid of being alone?"

"You're not listening—"

"Oh, I'm listening, all right. I'm listening to a man who presumes he has a right to me, a man who was willing to kidnap me to get what he wanted, and a man who held back not one, but two very important truths because he was afraid of rejection."

First the Santa thing, now the soulmate—helpmate—thing.

Once was forgivable, but twice? She crossed her arms over her chest and stepped away. The only reason to keep those things from her was because he didn't think her special enough to handle his secrets. And without trust, there could be no relationship. Better for her to leave before he could break her heart more.

"Lina—" He reached for her, but she backed away. His face fell, and he thrust his hands into his pockets.

"I want to go home now, please."

"Can I just try—"

"I want to go home."

"Please, you're breaking my heart. Don't do this."

"Breaking your heart? What about mine? What about me? You didn't give me a chance, Dash. You didn't give *us* a chance."

His brow furrowed and his body stiffened. "I gave us a chance. You're the one walking away."

Dash examined the toes of his boots for a moment, and all his softness and cheer melted away. When he looked up, the cool expression of a bartender greeted her, the one she'd only glimpsed the first night when he chatted with other customers. Every time he looked at her that night, and every day since, there'd been a spark of magic. It was gone now.

"Come on, I'll take you home." His voice was nearly devoid of all emotion.

He pulled the key out of his pocket and led her to the far end of the hall. A door glowed and he opened it. The hallway outside her sister's condo appeared.

"Lina, if there's anything I can do to make it up to you…"

"Don't hold your breath." She walked through the portal.

"If you change your mind, I'm just a phone call away," he said sadly.

She didn't look back, but a flash of blue light told her the gateway had vanished. Only then did she allow the tears to fall.

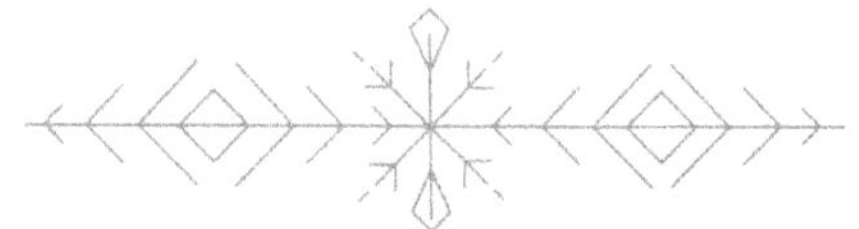

Chapter 23
Boxing Day Sucked

Christmas Day sucked.

Boxing Day sucked.

But Dash dragged his sorry ass out of bed the day after. He had been hoping she would call. She hadn't. Not a peep.

His mother had checked on him late Christmas afternoon, but she took one look at him and closed the door without a word.

He stumbled to the kitchen for coffee. Or maybe whiskey. It all depended upon what was available.

His father sat at the island, sipping a giant mug of coffee. He said nothing as Dash filled his own mug and joined him. The silence continued until his mother strode in a few minutes later.

"Good morning, Dash." She kissed his cheek.

He grunted, and his father shot him a dirty look.

"Leave him alone, Ivan. Can't you see his heart is broken?"

"It's his own damn fault. He lied to the poor girl. Twice!"

No truer words had ever been spoken. It was dangerous to become involved with humans. Not physically—emotionally. Yet he'd done it anyway.

"Ivan, we've talked about this. You're not allowed to be all judgmental when it comes to our children's love lives. Not anymore. They're adults."

"But—"

"He's right, Mom," Dash said. "It is my fault. I'm the wrong end of a reindeer and I deserve whatever I get."

"See, Katja, Dash even agrees with me."

"Only because he hasn't figured out how to win her back yet."

"I don't deserve to win her back," Dash muttered into his coffee.

His mom slung an arm around his shoulders. "Yes, you do. You love her, and I'm pretty sure she loves you. You're helpmates, after all."

"That's the problem. She doesn't believe in them, doesn't believe I love her."

His father stared at him as he polished off the coffee in his mug. Ivan rose and rummaged around in the pantry, pulling out a dusty bottle of brandy. He poured a measure into his mug and another in Dash's.

"Yeah, I don't believe in helpmates either," he said.

What?

Dash's expression must have said it all because his dad chuckled. Not the ho, ho, ho he was best known for, but an honest-to-goodness chuckle.

"Was I thrilled when you brought another human into our world? No, especially considering what happened with Victoria. Humans can be…unpredictable. I like Lina, from our two quick meetings, and if you told me earlier she was your helpmate, I wouldn't have been so grouchy to find her on the workshop floor on Christmas Eve."

His father's words struck him right in the heart, like an icicle falling from the eaves. Deep down, he knew he'd made a poor decision. No, he made a series of poor decisions. He was almost forty, and yet he was allowing his fear and his hormones to control him as much as they did when he was twenty.

"I know, Dad," he muttered.

"It took months for your mom to convince me we belonged together. Helpmates—bah, superstitious nonsense. Old stories to explain love at first sight, or to justify arranged marriages way back when. You become helpmates because you love and trust each other."

"But she doesn't trust me." *Not anymore.*

"Yeah, and whose fault is that?"

"Mine. I should have—"

"We can play shoulda, coulda, woulda until next Christmas, and it will fix nothing." Ivan glugged the brandy and poured some more. He held out the bottle to Dash, who shook his head. He hadn't finished what was in his cup yet.

Katja took the bottle from Ivan. "What your dad is trying to say is, what are you going to do to fix this?"

What could he do? He'd tried apologizing. Wait…he hadn't apologized. He'd *explained.* Thirty-nine years old and he was still a jackass.

"I'm going to apologize. Properly."

But it was only a few days until her sister's wedding. The last thing Lina needed to deal with right now was his shit.

"Good. And?" His dad peered at him over the rim of the mug.

"Hope she forgives me. That's all I can do."

"Oh, I think we can manage a grand gesture." His mom drank directly from the bottle of brandy before plonking it on the counter.

Joy skipped into the kitchen with a mischievous grin. "Or two."

She held up the ugliest, most magnificent, most wanted hat. Stripes of all colors and widths, no rhyme or reason to the pattern, topped with a giant green pom.

"How the hell did you find that?"

His sister tossed the hat to him. "It appeared in my bathroom sink this morning. You fucked up the spell. Don't tell me…you went counterclockwise in the circle instead of clockwise."

Yes, yes he had. Best. Fuckup. Ever.

"Language, Joy. Please," his mom said, but not as forcefully as she usually did.

"Sorry." She didn't look sorry, not one bit.

Reality sunk in. "She won't speak to me. I tried texting on Christmas."

"Of course she won't, reindeer brain." Joy nudged his shoulder. "But we can change her mind. Grand gesture, remember?"

"What the he—holly is a grand gesture?"

Out of the corner of his eye, he spotted his mother's thin lips, but her expression gleamed with…mischief? His *mother*?

"Read more romance, Dash. Somebody messes up, so they do a big, thoughtful *something*." Joy waved her arms wide.

"What, a big apology on the jumbotron at Fenway?"

She slapped the back of his head playfully and stole the bottle of brandy. Unlike their mother, she poured some into a glass.

"No, that's a cliché. Key word is thoughtful. You have her favorite hat. You want to return it to its rightful owner, so might as well add some flair."

Flair, huh? The best bartenders always put a little flair into their cocktails. He could do the same.

"Do you love her, Dash?" his mother asked from the other side of the kitchen. She distanced herself from the rest of her family, watching them with her kind, yet perceptive, eyes. "The best, most thoughtful, most spectacular gesture means nothing if you don't love her."

"She's my helpmate," he said, as if that answered her question.

His dad called him on his crap. "But do you *love* her? Can you imagine your life without her? If she wasn't your helpmate, would you still want her in your life? Because that's all a helpmate truly is—the person you want to be with most in the world."

His mother sidled over and kissed his father on the cheek. He grabbed her by the waist and pulled her on his lap, their laughter filling the kitchen.

Dash had always assumed if he had a helpmate, by definition, he would love her. He believed Lina was his helpmate, despite the fact she was human, despite the fact he'd known her two weeks, despite the fact she'd puked on his boots. And despite the fact he'd let her go.

Every time he thought of her, he lit up inside, as bright as Rudolph's nose, as clear as the sleigh bells on his father's sleigh, as infinite as the stars above the North Pole. Every time he was near her, he felt at peace, like a blanket of new-fallen snow. Every time he touched her, he warmed like the fires in all the hearths on Christmas Eve.

The notion of her not being a part of his life filled him with a sorrow as deep as a midwinter's night. He wanted nothing else than to be with her.

"Yes, I love her."

His mother's eyes twinkled, and his father's dimples made merry. She gently extricated herself from Ivan's embrace and bustled out of the kitchen, calling over her shoulder, "Then we have work to do!"

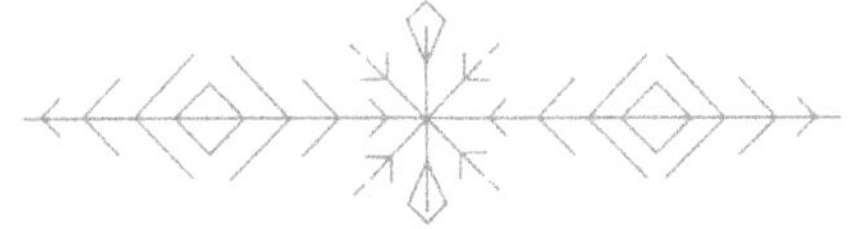

CHAPTER 24
SOME GRADE-A BULLSHIT

The only thing that kept Christmas Day from being a terrible, no good, fucking awful mess was Wesley's look of joy when he opened his gift and pulled out a facsimile of a granny hat. He put it on immediately, grinning from ear to ear.

"Where on Earth did you find this?" he asked, hugging her.

His parents looked on with carefully schooled faces. They didn't share their son's enthusiasm for ugly hats, but Lina's heart grew at least one size.

"Etsy, of course. Tiên ordered it ages ago. I made sure the colors clashed with Cassie's," she answered.

"Thank you, Lina. Now I feel like part of the family."

Her own parents beamed, and Cassie kept giggling whenever she glanced his way. But Wesley wore it with pride the whole day, even at dinner, despite the looks his parents kept sneaking his way. Yeah, her sister had chosen well.

The day after Christmas both sucked and blew. Lina didn't even get out of bed until noon. Everyone chalked it up to too much fine wine the night before, but she knew better. She had allowed a man she'd known less than a month to break her heart. He was supposed to be a fling. How had he wormed his way into her inner sanctum? But he had, she'd let him, and now she suffered the consequences of her own actions.

With the wedding less than a week away, she put on a brave face and pretended nothing was wrong. She fooled no one.

Lina picked up the phone to call him at least a dozen times. She missed his voice. She missed his texts. She missed his laugh.

Each time, she put the phone down, but she refused to block and delete his number. A small part of her hoped for his call. She would just yell at him again, but she hoped, nonetheless.

She'd never been anyone's first choice in high school, as much for her shyness as anything else. And since she put her career above everything, no one had cared enough to fight for her. Not even Dash.

She was no one's soulmate.

Three days before the wedding, Lina and her mother collected their dresses from the boutique. Lina's cheeks hurt from the fake smile she'd worn since Christmas Eve.

"What's wrong?" her mother asked as they waited for the salesperson to retrieve the altered dresses.

"Nothing, Mom."

"That's some grade-A bullshit."

"Mom!"

Her mother had become almost as foul-mouthed as a sailor since retirement.

"What? I don't have to put on an act for my children or my students anymore. I say what I want. But you, my dear, are holding back."

"It's fine. I'd rather not ruin Cassie's day."

"And this frightening fake smile won't?"

Busted. "I'm practicing so it doesn't look so ghoulish on New Year's, okay?"

The salesperson returned with the two dresses. They walked out of the store and hailed a rideshare. No one wanted to risk the gowns on the T, especially not with the wintry drizzle falling.

Cassie would sympathize. Her sister was a kind person. She would not hold Lina's broken heart against her at the wedding. In fact, she would make sure Lina had something—or someone—to distract her.

The sad fact was, Lina desired no one else. Although he had betrayed her, apparently it wasn't enough to banish him from her thoughts, the rotten bastard.

"You don't have to be anything you don't want to be Lina, not to keep your family happy. We love you, even when you're sad," her mom said as the elevator doors closed on the ground floor of the high rise.

"But this is Cassie's wedding." Lina punched the button for Cassie's floor. "I won't make this about me."

Even the elevator doors reminded her of Dash. Would she ever walk through a door without thinking of him?

Her mom studied her with a keen intelligence that had taken the measure of thousands of bad faith arguments from her students, had picked out plagiarism instantly, and had recognized the genuine stars in her classes.

"Fine, but if you change your mind…"

"I know where to find you. Got it."

The elevator doors opened and Lina once again plastered her smile on. Just a few more days. The rehearsal was the day after tomorrow, then the wedding. And two days later, she would be on a plane to Greece and could put this all behind her.

She read snug in bed all the next day, only coming out for caffeine and food. She didn't even bother to take a shower or change out of her flannel pajamas, and she refused to meet Cassie's pitying gaze. Neither she nor Wes had asked what was wrong, though she could see the concern in their expressions when she scurried back to her room.

Some soul searching might be the best course to take in these strange liminal days between Christmas and New Year's, but whenever her mind veered toward Dash, all she found was heartache with a sprinkling of anger. She'd had high hopes, and he'd flung them into the slush by not being honest with her.

Yet…she couldn't get him off her mind. He hovered there, almost magically, behind her eyelids whenever she closed them. His voice echoed in her ears, though she hadn't heard a peep from him in days. And his scent, the strange mixture of snow and evergreen and mint, was tantalizingly out of reach. She missed him, and she was angry at him, and she was frightened about what it all could mean.

It rained again on the way to the rehearsal the next day, washing away the snow and dragging Lina's mood even further into the gutter. Her clothes were damp, and she slipped on the floor as she entered the venue, nearly face-planting into a bench and making an utter fool of herself.

The friend of the family who had agreed to officiate was late and arrived covered in slush a car had splashed on her. Cassie's heel broke, and Wesley lost a glove. No clue where it went—one second it was there, the next, poof. Her dad let out a loud burp as the bride and groom practiced their vows. And Lina overheard Wesley's mom snapping at the catering staff over the phone about some snafu with the starter course.

Lina collapsed on one of the folding chairs set up for them after they were done. She leaned back and stared at the vaulted ceiling, which only reminded her of the view from the boardroom at the North Pole. She could be looking at the aurora borealis tonight instead of the lovely, but far less awe-inspiring, ceiling of a wedding venue.

"Well, they say a bad dress rehearsal means a good opening night, right?" Cassie plopped beside her, far too chipper for Lina's liking. She rested her head on Lina's shoulder.

"That's for theater, Cass, not weddings."

"Potato, po-tah-to. This is all a big performance. What matters is I show up, Wesley shows up, and the officiant signs the document. The rest is just for kicks."

"You need witnesses, too."

"Yeah, yeah. I am a lawyer, you know." She straightened and slung her arm around Lina. "Speaking of which, one of the secrets we keep from non-lawyers is that there's a special law school class on spotting lying liars. And you, dear sister, are the lying-est liar I've spotted this year."

"They do not have a class on that." Lina leaned into her sister's embrace.

"No, they don't, but I know when you're out of sorts and trying to hide it. I am, after all, also your sister."

"It's fine."

"Lina, the last time you used that tone of voice and told me everything was fine, it was when your luggage got lost on the way to my law school graduation. What happened with Dash?"

"I will not be the person responsible for ruining your wedding day." Lina tried to rise, but Cassie held on tight. Lina was both frustrated and touched.

"The only thing that can ruin my wedding day is if my groom doesn't show. Everything else can be fixed. The question is, can whatever happened between you and Dash be fixed?"

Could it? He'd semi-kidnapped her and withheld the truth from her. But the way he looked at her made her feel seen in a way few had. Made her feel desired in a way few had. Made her feel loved in a way none had.

She had worked long and hard to accept who she was, and Dash had done so without reservation. Perhaps that was why she was touchy. She didn't trust his emotions were genuine, and the half-truths he'd fed her before played into her distrust.

"I don't know."

"Did he lie, cheat, or steal?"

Had he? He'd withheld important truths, misled her, but she'd given him a second chance because who would believe she was dating the son of Santa Claus? But outright lie? No.

As for cheating, would introducing her to magic reindeer be considered a shortcut to winning a woman's heart? Probably, but that wasn't what Cassie meant. From all Dash had told her about helpmates, he would never cheat.

But he had stolen her heart. She couldn't forgive that. Could she?

"He believes in soulmates and thinks I'm his."

Cassie blinked at her and paused a bit too long in her response.

"You're upset because he believes you're his soulmate," she said in a carefully neutral voice, her best lawyer voice. The same voice her father used when ferreting out the truth from a couple of teenage girls.

She couldn't very well admit it was more than that. She was upset because…because…

"I only found out because I overheard him tell his dad." *Yes, stick to that.* Dash refused to reveal the truth about any of it until she caught him out. And he hadn't even apologized, just tried to explain away his shitty behavior. She was angry, but her anger was becoming harder to hold on to the longer she was apart from him.

"He withheld the truth about falling in love with you at first sight, and that's why you're mad? What if he had told you he loved you when you went back for your hat? That would have been wicked creepy."

She hated when her sister called her out on her crap. Lina expected her mother to do so, but her little sister? Beyond embarrassing.

"Fine, make sense, but it's not your heart on the line."

"Not every man is like the assholes who went to our high

school, Lina. From what you've told me, Dash is a good guy. I mean, he fell for you despite you puking on him. If that doesn't speak to his character, I don't know what will. He may not be a Wesley, but he's certainly worth a second chance."

"I gave him one, and he blew it."

"By not confessing his undying love two weeks into dating?"

"Ugh." Lina broke away from Cassie and paced in front of the row of chairs. "You don't understand."

The more she talked to her sister, the less Lina understood herself.

"You're right, I don't. You finally found someone worthy of you, and you're pissed he loves you."

"He hasn't said that."

"He said you were his soulmate, right?"

Lina bit her lip and nodded.

"He'll get there. But I'm pulling another Dad, and here's your question. Will you? Don't answer yet, think about it, because here's my observation. You, my wicked smart, brave, and beautiful sister, are scared."

"Am not!"

Cassie did her best impression of their father's *you're lying* face—a sly quirk to her mouth, lowered brows, and an intense glare that shot straight into Lina's soul. Jesus.

"I'm gonna let you sit with that for a bit," Cassie said after a minute. "Imagine how you want to start the New Year—you can cling to your past or you can accept a different future. I love you, Lina. So do Mom and Dad and Wesley. Tiên does, too, and you've made some great friends in your work. You deserve love, and you deserve Dash. If you agree, call him before midnight tomorrow. If you don't, then don't. Get on the plane in a few days and go back to how things were."

Dammit, dammit, dammit. Her sister was making sense. She was scared. Terrified, if she were being honest. Dash was everything she could wish for in a partner. Loving, great sense of humor, an ass to rival Chris Evans's. He had a job he loved and kept him busy. And a magic key that could take him anywhere in the world. Long-distance had little meaning for the Nichols family.

She could have everything she ever wanted if she was brave enough to take the next step.

Wesley joined them, kissing the top of Cassie's head. "Sorry to interrupt, but they're kicking us out. It's getting late, and we've got a big day tomorrow."

Cassie rose and kissed him on the cheek before turning her knowing eyes on Lina. "Think about it, Lina. Actually, no, don't think about it. You've done way too much of that already. Feel it, let your heart guide you. You have a good one. Listen to it for once, for fuck's sake."

CHAPTER 25
WICKED EARLY

Dash stepped through the doorway in an empty service hall of the hotel, carrying a smallish box that fit perfectly in his hands. It was wrapped in white paper with swirls of gold glitter. Sheer gold ribbon twists adorned the top, and a simple white tag read, "Lina."

"Hey, you can't be back here," a tuxedoed server said as Dash rounded a corner.

"Sorry, man, got turned around. Where is the Schultz-Blackworth wedding reception?"

"You're wicked early."

"Yeah, just have a delivery." Dash raised the box.

"Sure, follow me."

The man led him past the smaller hall set up for the wedding itself and into a large ballroom decorated in black, white, and gold. Round tables with black linens held arrangements of white roses in tall, thin, golden vases. Fairy lights were hung with abandon, sparkling off the glasses, the silverware, and the white place settings.

"Who is the delivery for?" the server asked.

"Maid of honor."

"Head table's there." He gestured at the long, rectangular table at the far end of the room. "There are place cards, so if you know her name, should be easy."

The server didn't leave as Dash's boots tromped through the venue. He hadn't dressed the part, wearing jeans and a dark green cable-knit sweater. As he glanced around, a small part of him pictured what his wedding would look like. He was not one to care about these things—he enjoyed celebrating the happiness of his friends and family, but after Victoria, he had never imagined a walk down the aisle.

Dash shoved the images into a vault of wishful thinking. He had no idea if Lina would accept his apology. Yet visions of her in various wedding dresses popped into his mind. A sundress on a beach. A ballgown in the boardroom. A pantsuit in a town hall. Any venue she wanted, any dress she wanted, any day she wanted, he would be there wearing a smile and his best suit, knowing he was the luckiest elf on the entire planet.

And if she never wanted, well, he would have to accept that. He was a patient man. Okay, he wouldn't lie to himself. He was impatient. The best thing in his life had walked into his bar nineteen days ago, and he wanted nothing more than to cherish her. Honor her. Love her. It was out of his hands. All he could do was give her his heart. And her ugly-ass hat.

He found her name next to her sister's and placed the box on her chair. It was never a good idea to upset the aesthetic at a high society wedding. His mother hadn't raised a fool.

"All done, sir?" The server looked at his phone. "Do you need to check in with the bridal party? They should be here in about half an hour."

"No. This is it."

He trudged across the dance floor. One day, he hoped to see Lina dance again, hoped to hold her in his arms as she did. Dash doubted today would be that day, but if everything went according to plan, the day would come.

The server closed the door behind them and walked him to the front of the hotel.

"Thanks," Dash said as he slipped out the front doors.

He turned a corner and found a quiet alley and a locked door. He went home and poured himself a stiff drink. Nothing to do now but wait.

Chapter 26
All Sparkly and Bright

Fat snowflakes drifted out of the low gray clouds as Lina carefully skirted the puddles leftover from yesterday's rain. An expectant hush hung in the air, broken by the women surrounding her. The giggling gaggle of bridesmaids flocked into the hotel, dress bags slung over shoulders and heels carried in hand, arranged protectively around Cassie.

They took the elevator to the suite Lina's parents had reserved. Bottles of water waited, as did a bottle of champagne with some plastic flutes. Her sister was smart—no drunk bridesmaids before the reception. After a quick toast, they got to work.

Lina slid into her dress, a gold confection with a sweetheart neckline and a chiffon overlay with gold leaves. It hugged every one of her curves, and she gleamed like a Christmas ornament, in the best way possible. All sparkly and bright, something to admire and reflect joy to the onlooker. Too bad her insides were a dark pit of despair, confusion, and loss.

Despite her sister's advice, Lina still hadn't made up her mind about Dash. But she had a revelation during her restless night. She *was* scared, damn her sister for being right. Scared he wanted too much, scared she would be too little. Lina hated being scared. She may not be the most gregarious person in the world, preferring a night in with friends or a good book, but she worked in war zones and waded through the aftermath of natural disasters for a living. Carolina Schultz feared nothing. Except, apparently, love. Or the possibility of it.

So, the question remained, was she brave enough to take a final chance on Dash? Thus far, she'd been unable to answer that question. One minute, her heart told her yes. The next, her head screamed no.

Two hours later, she was still undecided, but her hair was coiffed, her makeup on point, and she held a beautiful bouquet of white roses wrapped in black ribbon. Gold leaf edged a single rose. Holy crap, this was some serious disposable income. She always knew Wesley's parents were loaded, but this was some next level fuckery. No wonder they had met her Christmas gift to him with polite indifference.

But as beautiful as Lina felt, Cassie took home the gold medal. Her dress was similar in style to the bridesmaids' dresses but had a short train. Black lace overlay the creamy wedding dress. Every rose in her bouquet was limned in gold, and a gold ribbon wrapped the stems.

Cassie went with a natural look and wore a classic chignon dotted with gold roses. Her mother's pearl earrings hung from her ears, and a simple pearl pendant finished the outfit. Cassie glowed with excitement and love. She was breathtaking, the way a bride should be.

Someone knocked on the door, and Lina answered. Her dad stood outside.

"Everyone ready? We have about thirty minutes until showtime."

"Yeah, we're all decent."

Tears welled in her father's eyes as he found Cassie standing on the far side of the room. He walked over and hugged her, careful not to damage her hair or makeup.

"I'm proud of you, sweetheart. Not because you're getting married; god knows that's not an accomplishment for a woman. But because you're you, and I don't tell you often enough."

"Thanks, Dad." Cassie beamed, and glowed, and did all the things a bride was supposed to do on her wedding day.

He turned to Lina. "And I'm proud of you, too. Whether I ever walk you down the aisle or not, as long as you're happy, I'm happy."

She rushed into his arms and repeated her sister's words. "Thanks, Dad."

The gaggle pulled out tissues and carefully dabbed at their tears. He took a small box from his coat and presented it to Cassie.

"It was your granny's. I know she'd want you to wear it today."

She opened it. Resting on some tissue paper was a gold charm bracelet, the one their granny always donned on family occasions. There was the watering can, signifying their grandmother and her love of gardening. The airplane for grandpa, who had been an Air Force pilot. Scales for their dad, and a book for their mom. Lina's was a working bell, and Cassie's was a flower. A new one, bright and shiny, caught her attention. A baseball bat for Wesley, who took Cassie to a Red Sox game for their first date.

"Let me." Lina plucked it out of the box and fastened it around her sister's wrist.

It tinkled, a softer version of the bells on Santa's sleigh.

"Just a reminder you'll always have your family with you, no matter where your adventures take you," Dad said.

"You're going to make me cry and ruin my mascara." Cassie fanned her face with her hand.

Lina offered her a tissue a split second before the other bridesmaids all jumped to do the same.

"Are you ready?" Her dad offered his elbow.

Cassie hooked her arm through his, and they all paraded out of the room and to the venue. Some last-minute shuffling outside the doors, then the music started. Cassie and Wesley had made a deal with his parents—they would have a classy string quartet as long as they were allowed to choose the music.

The opening notes of "Sweet Child o' Mine" floated through the air as the staff threw open the doors. Her first genuine smile pulled up the corners of Lina's mouth as she followed the other bridesmaids down the aisle. Wesley's parents looked on with thinned lips, but Wesley himself grinned from ear to ear. His brown eyes reflected the fairy lights hanging from the walls and ceiling, giving him a magical, almost an elvish, air.

Tiên happily waggled her fingers at her as Lina took her place and waited for her sister.

Cassie walked in, escorted by both her parents, one on each arm. The patriarchy stood little chance in the Schultz household, with her mother teaching women's history and her father specializing in sexual harassment lawsuits, so both parents would bless this union.

Lina snuck a glance at Wesley. He'd been Cassie's friendly rival their first year of law school, always challenging her. She challenged him right back, and they drove each other to be the best in their class. Two months after graduation, he finally asked her on a date to Fenway. Wesley looked at her sister with humor, love, and occasional desire, though Lina wished she could erase *those* memories.

But now, he looked upon her baby sister with devotion, awe, and yes, love. A love deep enough, broad enough to stand everything the years would throw at them. It flowed through the room, permeating the air and infusing those gathered with peace and joy. If only someone looked at *her* with that kind of love.

That's when it hit her like a truck barreling down the Pike. *Dash* had looked at her like that. And she'd missed it. When he ordered her lunch and knew strawberry frappes were her favorite. When he kissed her, the same awe had shone from his gaze. And when she woke next to him, peace and joy filled her, which only came from finding a soulmate. Helpmate. Whatever.

Well, fuck.

She owed Dash a phone call. As soon as the major festivities were over, Lina would do it. She'd be brave and confront her fear. Love was on the line, and it was worth the risk.

The ceremony proceeded according to plan. Cassie was right—a bad dress rehearsal boded well for the big event. Nothing went awry. Everyone said their lines right on cue, and before long, Wesley kissed Cassie like there was no tomorrow to the hoots and whistles of most of the guests. Lina would even swear under oath Mr. and Mrs. Blackworth smiled.

She and the best man stayed to sign the certificate while the rest of the guests filed to the reception hall.

"Thanks, sis," Wesley said with the biggest, goofiest smile.

"Ugh, don't ever call me that again."

"Whatever you say, sis." He kissed her cheek.

Cassie squealed and hugged her close.

"I have a phone call to make as soon as we get a moment," Lina whispered.

"I'm happy for you. Now, let's drink. I have to talk to Wesley's extended family today. They never talk about anything fun, so the only way I will enjoy myself is with copious amounts of alcohol."

"They're not that bad," Wesley protested, taking his wife's hand in his.

Cassie kissed her husband. "No, they're worse, but it's okay. I'll talk lawyer to them every day for the next fifty years as long as you're there."

"You're going to give me a cavity if you keep it up." Lina rolled her eyes but couldn't keep the smile away.

"Someday this will be you, Lina, sooner than you think."

"Oh?" Wesley looked at her with a strange gleam in his eye. "Something happen with Hottie McBartender?"

"Never let those words pass your lips again, and I might tell you." Lina gave his shoulder a playful shove.

"Deal. I knew it was wrong the moment I said it."

Laughing, they walked down the hall to the grand ballroom. Lina slipped in and gave the cue to the quartet. "Thunderstruck" played. Her dad laughed, but Wesley's parents looked less than pleased. Their own fault for making a deal with two young lawyers. The quartet played with gusto and wide grins, having the time of their lives.

Lina walked to the head table. Wesley escorted Cassie through the tables to the sound of applause and laughter. An auspicious beginning to this new phase of their lives.

Finally, they arrived at the head table and everyone sat. Everyone except Lina. On her chair was a beautifully wrapped box, about the size of a large book.

"What is it, Lina?" Cassie asked when she didn't sit.

"Did you get me a present?"

Cassie's gaze traveled to the box. "Nope. Is it ticking?"

The tag had her name on it in bright red flowing letters, but she did not recognize the writing. She picked up the box. It was light, and the contents shifted as she shook it gently. Lina held it to her ear.

She finally sat, placing the box to the side. "No ticking."

"Aren't you going to open it?"

"It'll keep."

"You should open it, Lina," Wesley piped in. "Cassie doesn't like surprises. She won't be able to concentrate on anything until you open the box."

"He's right. Open it." Her sister's eyes flashed wildly as she tapped her fingers on the table.

A dozen servers came out, carrying trays of wine flutes and bottles of champagne.

"After the toasts, I promise," Lina said as a server filled her glass.

Her mother went first, followed by Wesley's father, both making short work of their parts, wishing the bride and groom nothing but joy and happiness. Lina and the best man had flipped a coin to decide who would go last. He lost. Thankfully there were no kids tonight; he spent his toast wishing them lots of sex. Which wasn't a bad wish, but read the room, dude.

Then it was Lina's turn. She stood and glanced at her sister before looking over the crowd.

"Once upon a time, Mom and Dad brought home a baby, who promptly cried when I poked her. I had no idea she would turn out to be my best friend. That took about fifteen years and gallons of ice cream."

Chuckles drifted through the room.

"But here we are, twenty-eight years, nine months, and eleven days later, and I've never been happier for her. Cassie, Wesley, you are lucky to have each other, and I love you. May your home offer comfort, may your table be full, and may you always look at each other with the same love I see today. Cheers!"

Cassie hugged her. "Now open the goddamned gift."

"Who am I to deny a bride's wish on her wedding day?"

Lina sat again, and the servers brought out the main course. She pulled the ribbon off and carefully opened the package. A folded note rested on top of red tissue paper, written in a different hand than the tag.

Dear Lina,

Joy found this after Christmas. I wasn't sure you'd want to hear from me again, but you need your granny hat back.

I owe you an apology.

I am sorry. You were right. I was so afraid of losing you, I didn't trust you with the truth. I didn't even trust myself with it. And here it is—

I loved you from the moment you walked into my bar with this ridiculous hat on. I loved you when you puked on my boots. I loved you when you kissed me. I loved you when you were mad. I loved you under the aurora borealis. I loved you in my bed. I loved you when you delivered presents to sick kids.

I love you, Lina. Whether we are fated to be together or it was pure, magical luck, I will love you always. And if you love me too, if you ever forgive me, there's a little something extra under the hat. You can find me anytime, anywhere, if it takes a day, a month, or a decade.

Love always, Dash

P.S. There's one more thing. My given name isn't Dash. It's Ivan. Ivan Feliks Nichols. You now have all my secrets.

Wrapped in the red tissue paper was a bright monstrosity of a winter hat, complete with green pom.

"Is that—"

"Granny's hat."

Her sister elbowed her. "Told you Dash was a keeper."

"How do you know it's from Dash?"

"You have the silliest grin on your face right now, Lina. Who else is it going to be from? So, you going to call him?"

"Call who?" asked Wesley.

"Dash," said Cassie.

"Oh, yeah, you should call him, Lina. He's a good guy. I looked into him a bit. His company has profit sharing with his employees, and he donates a hundred thousand dollars to charity each year. Makes no fuss about it, just donates. Children's charities, mostly."

"Wait a minute, there's something else in here," Lina said.

Carefully, almost with reverence, she took out her granny hat and put it on the table. Underneath was a finely wrought silver skeleton key. The bit was in the shape of a snowflake.

"What's that?" Cassie asked.

"Magic," Lina said. Silence fell over the table as she ignored her food.

"Hey Lina." Cassie poked her in the shoulder.

"Yes?"

"Why are you still here?"

"It's your wedding."

"And nothing would make me happier than for my sister to find her happily ever after on my wedding day. Find him. If there's enough time, bring him here and kiss him at midnight."

Lina looked at Wesley.

"I am not going to argue with my wife on our wedding day."

Grabbing the key and the hat, Lina stood and rushed out. All eyes followed her, but she didn't care. She could explain later, or Cassie would. This moment was her chance at what Cassie had, and she wasn't going to waste it.

Footsteps followed her into the hall.

"Lina, wait. What's wrong?" Tiên called after her.

Lina stopped, allowing her friend to catch up. "Nothing's wrong. In fact, everything's right."

"I see someone found your granny hat. Would that someone happen to be a bartender?"

Lina couldn't keep the wide grin from her lips. "Maybe."

Tiên arched an eyebrow.

"Okay, yes, it's Dash. He found it, he apologized, and now I'm going to find him."

"Hon, the exit's that way." Tiên pointed toward the vast hotel lobby.

"Not for me." At her friend's confusion, Lina said, "It's a long, unbelievable story. I'll tell you someday over tropical drinks. But I have to go."

When love struck this hard, when the decision to move past fear was made, it was time to act.

"I'm happy for you." Tiên threw her arms around Lina, holding her tight for a moment before snagging the hat from her hands. Tiên shoved the cap on Lina's head and gently pushed her in the direction she'd been going. "That's better. Now, go."

Lina ran through the hotel, looking for a door no one was using. There was a utilitarian stairwell at the end of the catering wing. She held the key out to the door. A glowing keyhole appeared, and she opened the gateway.

The blue glow disappeared, leaving only the merry light of a fire to guide her. Dash sat in a chair facing the door, and the most wondrous smile spread across his lips as she stepped through.

"You got my note," he said, standing.

She pointed at the hat. "Thank you. How did you find it?"

He slowly crossed the floor. "Magic, but it went a little awry. It appeared in my sister's room instead of mine."

He stood an arm's length from her, and an expectant air perfumed the room.

Lina held out the key. "I thought only elves could use these."

Dash closed her fingers around it. A shiver of anticipation ran through her.

"Usually, but this key is special. It will bring you to wherever I am."

She stepped closer. His soft scent of wintergreen and snow wrapped her in an embrace.

"Wherever you are?" Her voice dropped, and his pupils dilated.

"Yes. I never want to be more than a doorway from you. Not today, not tomorrow, not ever."

"Not ever sounds good to me."

"It does?"

"Yes."

They stood for a minute, staring at each other, holding their breaths, waiting. Lina broke first.

"Dash?"

"Yes?"

"Why aren't you kissing me yet?"

"I thought you'd never ask."

He snaked an arm around her waist and pulled her tight. Running his fingers through her hair, he tilted her head up to him and lowered his lips to hers. His breath was icy sweet, and his tongue teased her lips. She opened for him and brushed her tongue along his lower lip.

A growl rumbled in his chest, and she smiled under his kiss.

"I love you, Lina," he said.

"I love you too, Dash. So much it scared me. You're too good to be true."

"No, I messed up, but I will spend the rest of my life making it up to you, if you'll let me."

"I let my fear get the best of me. I won't do that again. We'll figure out a way to make it up to each other."

"That sounds like the best idea I've heard all week."

"I have another one." Lina looked at the key still clutched in her palm. "You see, there's this New Year's party going on, and I want to dance with you, Ivan Feliks Nichols."

His eyes twinkled in the firelight as he looked her over. "As long as you promise to never call me that again, I will be happy to dance with you, Carolina Schultz. I will be the luckiest man there, dancing with the prettiest woman. Have I mentioned you are divine in this dress?"

"You will be the second luckiest man, and no one is ever more beautiful than the bride. But you can compliment me on this dress anytime."

"I stand corrected."

"How did you end up with Dash out of Ivan?" she asked, still nervous.

"My grandfather decided I was as fast and as smart as his favorite reindeer." Dash's expression was carefully neutral.

"His favorite—he named you after Dasher?" Her hand flew to her mouth to hide her wide grin.

"Go ahead and laugh. It's ridiculous, but I like it a helluva a lot better than Ivan." But he smiled as he said it.

She tapped his nose with her finger. "I do, too."

He grabbed her finger and brought her hand to his lips, placing a tender kiss on the back. He claimed her mouth again, dropping her hand to allow his to roam over her curves. Dash squeezed her ass and ran his fingers along the edges of the dress, teasing and tickling her skin. With a low groan, he broke away.

"If we don't go now, we're not going anywhere."

Lina smiled slyly and took his arm.

"Promises, promises."

He pulled out his key and took her back to the wedding, where they danced the night away and kissed at midnight. Lina could have sworn she heard sleigh bells ringing.

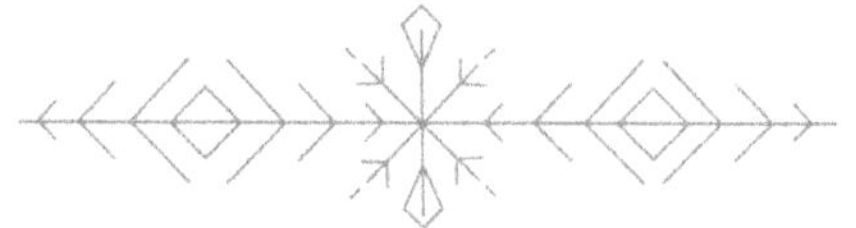

EPILOGUE
ONE YEAR LATER

Dash stepped through the door, the last of the presents under the tree at his last house this Christmas Eve. With her recent reassignment to the international aid organization's Washington, DC, headquarters, Lina wasn't able to make it tonight. She had to work today but had the next week off. Though distance wasn't an issue for them, he was glad she was going to be closer to her family for at least a few years.

They'd soon have to have an important conversation about secrets, reindeer, and the North Pole with the Schultzes. At least now that his dad had finally given Joy the responsibilities she deserved, Dash had more time to develop those relationships. He often joined Cassie and Wesley for dinner.

He strolled through the halls, whistling that damn song by Mariah Carey. Until he met Lina, it had annoyed the ever-living snowflakes out of him. But ever since she walked into his bar, he couldn't think of a better Christmas song.

Hundreds of elves passed him, eagerly vanishing into the main distribution center for the after-hours cocoa bar, an annual tradition instituted by his mother. As much as he wanted to join them, he was tired and hoped to call Lina before she drifted off to sleep tonight.

He pulled out his phone—it was after two in the morning Eastern time. Crap, he would have to wait. Between the busy Christmas season and her new assignment, it had been a few weeks since they'd had time for more than a few quick phone calls and some flirty texts. At least he'd see her soon. She promised to come over as soon as she got up on Christmas morning. Maybe he could convince her to wear only her red scarf.

Dash opened the door to his room and stopped in his tracks. Candles adorned every flat surface—his dresser, the nightstands, the coffee table, the mantel. A fire flickered in the hearth, and two filled martini glasses sat on the coffee table, the candy canes sticking out and slowly dissolving. But what truly made him stop and hold his breath was the vision of loveliness asleep in his bed.

Lina rested on top of the covers, dressed in a sheer black robe. A red ribbon tied it closed, finished with a beautiful bow. Under the robe, she wore a matching bra and panty set in the same red as the bow. The fuzzy blanket she'd gifted him last year covered her toes. His cock stirred. No matter how tired he was, he was not too tired for this. But she might be.

Cautiously and quietly, he walked to the bed and sat next to her.

"Hi, gorgeous," he murmured, brushing her cheek.

She blinked and trained her Christmas tree eyes on him. "I'm sorry. Did I fall asleep?"

He cupped her cheek. "Yes, but if you're tired, I can tuck you in."

"I am not too tired for you. I got all dressed up, convinced Joy to come get me. Even wore a bow."

"I was the one supposed to be wearing a bow."

She grasped his hand and slid it down her body to rest on the curve of her breast. "Next year." She grinned devilishly.

He kissed the grin right off her face, drinking in her low moans, reveling in her softness. Dash trailed his hand over her side to her hip, and she shivered beneath his touch.

Lina tipped her head back, and he kissed his way down her neck. He nibbled at her collarbone and slipped his hand under the hem of her robe. He walked his fingers up her thick thigh and slid them over her pussy. She was already soaked.

"Lie back," he said.

She did, and he untied his present, gently pushing the gauzy material off her body.

"How did I get so lucky?" he murmured.

"Because you are a very, very nice boy."

He clamped his lips on her nipple through the lacy bra, and Lina arched into him, running her fingers through his hair and holding him to her. Dash circled his arms around and undid the clasp, freeing her beautiful, full breasts. He pulled down the edge and licked her nipple. She bucked against him.

"Like that?"

"You know I do."

"Yes, I do." He closed his teeth gently over the hard nub, and a hushed groan filled the space between them. All he wanted was to bury himself deep in her and never leave.

Dash pulled his sweater off and flicked open the button on his jeans. She pushed away his hands and undid the zipper, stroking him through his boxer-briefs. He hissed in a breath.

"Like that?" She turned his own words against him.

With a growl, he grabbed her wrists and held them over her head. "You know I do."

She arched under him, rubbing her wet pussy against his hard cock.

"Damn, what you do to me, Lina."

She licked her lips, slowly, seductively. He bent and kissed her, sucking her pretty pink tongue into his mouth. She molded her body to his, but it wasn't enough. It never would be.

He let go of her wrists and stood, kicking off his shoes and dropping his jeans and underwear in a smooth motion. His cock stood at attention, waiting, wanting.

"Take off the underwear," he said.

Lina sat up and started slipping off the robe.

"No, leave the robe."

She smiled and bit her lower lip as she shimmied out of her bra and panties. He knelt before her and kissed her pussy, sucking on her clit while sliding in a finger. So wet, and all for him. She lifted her hips.

He reached for the condoms he kept in the nightstand. Lina grabbed his wrist.

"I got the birth control implants two weeks ago. We're good."

Fuck yes. He wasted no more time. Dash lifted her legs and wrapped them around his waist. Then he buried himself in her. Their groans mingled in the firelight as he moved in and out, supporting her hips with one arm while using his other hand to rub her clit.

She tossed her head in ecstasy and thumbed her nipples. Her moan turned to mewling as she writhed under him, lost in her pleasure. Watching her lose control brought him to the edge, and he stayed there, hovering on the cusp of diving into bliss. He refused to come before she did.

"Eyes on me, angel," he ground out.

Her eyes popped open, following the trail down his chest to where they were joined.

"Come for me, Lina."

She splintered, sending him over the edge. Swirls of color filled the air. He never tired of it—their gentle beauty reminded him how much a gift their love was.

Dash helped her get comfortable before going to the

bathroom and cleaning himself up. He brought out a warm washcloth and took care of Lina. Finally, tired and satiated, he clambered into bed over her, rolling her into his arms.

"Merry Christmas. I love you, Dash." She kissed his cheek.

"Merry Christmas, I love you, too."

They drifted off to sleep, Dash smiling to himself about the small box with a star sapphire ring waiting in his closet, enchanted to extend her lifespan to that of an elf's. He had grand plans for this New Year's Eve. Grand plans for the rest of their lives.

THE END

Experience Cassie's first date with Wesley in "Pushing the Clock," a short story available only to newsletter subscribers. You'll also get the magical chocolate-mint martini recipe.

www.EmilyMichelAuthor.com/newsletter

ACKNOWLEDGMENTS

First off, a shout out to my brother Eric, bartender extraordinaire, for the help with the bartending stuff in this book, like the wine Dash ordered in the Italian restaurant and the chocolate-mint martini recipe. And congrats on the promotion. If you're ever in Tucson, stop by the Kingfisher and say hi to him. Any mistakes about bartending are entirely my own.

I'd be remiss if I didn't acknowledge the wonderful podcast *Pop Culture Happy Hour*. I've been a regular listener for a decade, catching up on what's going on with movies, TV, music, and books. And about two weeks before Christmas of 2022, they had a roundtable discussion on the movie *Violent Nights*. Someone mentioned a scene in the movie where Santa is nearly black-out drunk, and that caught my attention.

A scene popped in my head of a Santa waking up after a hard night of partying, and I couldn't get it off my mind (the bones are in the "No Fucking Tiaras" chapter). I sat down two Fridays before Christmas and wrote. By Sunday night, I had ten thousand words. It wasn't dark at all, and the characters just spoke to me and through me. Six weeks later, the manuscript of a book I didn't plan on writing was complete.

And here you have it. I have written my first romcom. No one dies. The angst is low, the sugar content is high, and it's relatively spicy, too. It may be my only romcom, but it sure was a fun ride.

This book wouldn't be as good as it is without my wonderful beta readers, Ciara, Nia, JA, and Nicole. The incomparable Gail Delaney, my editor, is quick, kind, and thorough, and offered some great feedback on New England slang (she grew up there, while I only stayed a couple years). She gives me the reality checks and the encouragement I need.

As always, I'd like to thank my husband. None of this would be possible without him. My kids, too, who put up with my space cadet ways and listen to me babble about things like grammar and story and marketing. The snots keep getting older, and I treasure these moments before they fly the coop.

If you like this book, take a minute to drop some stars or leave a review at a retailer of your choice or one of the book review websites. It will help other readers find books they like and can give an author a much-needed mood boost.

KICKSTARTER BACKERS

Reindeer Wranglers

Pam Smith and Michele Johnson - Stanley

Backers

Abby A
Annette M
Anonymous Reader
Becky C
Brianna Welch-Martin
Bridget C
Christine D
David Neth
Eric Martin
Eric Smith
Jessica Beckendorf
Kathy Brady
Katie Slagle
L Simpson
Lesley G
Liz Alden
Liz Zerkel
Lori S
Melanie P
Melissa F Miller
Nijeara "Ny" Buie
Peg Perl
PunkARTchick RAD
Rosie Pease
Shrug Emoji
Stephanie K Clemens
Summer G
TL Ryder
Yvonne Z

ABOUT THE AUTHOR

Emily Michel is a middle-aged woman who didn't realize telling herself bedtime stories was a weird thing to do until her thirties. Since then, she's written many books, collected more cats and bookmarks, trained two drivers, and raised one whole-ass adult. When she's not at her computer, she's reading, crocheting, watching TV, and trying to find snacks. Occasionally, her husband drags her out of the house for her own good. You can find her on many social media platforms with the handle @EmiMiWriter. She is most active on TikTok. For links to everything (like, everything, everything) and to sign up to her newsletter go to www.emilymichelauthor.com.

OTHER BOOKS BY EMILY MICHEL

Magic & Monsters Series

Annie isn't afraid of the things that go bump in the night, but Rhys can't let her face the monsters alone. Complete paranormal romance trilogy with a powerful witch new to her magic, a morally gray hero, and a second chance at love.

Witch Hazel & Wolfsbane
Devil's Claw & Moonstone
Brimstone & Silver

The Memory Duology

How far will Hell's top hitman go to save the angel he was sent to kill? A complete paranormal romance duo with a slow burn, enemies to lovers, and a redemption arc.

A Memory of Wings
A Redemption of Wings

The Lorean Tales

A series of interconnected standalone fairy tale retellings. Book 1 is a gender-flipped Snow White reimagining.

Blood Magic and Brandy
Books 2 & 3 coming in 2024

Milton Keynes UK
Ingram Content Group UK Ltd.
UKHW010249221123
432980UK00005B/450